"Are you sure you need to say no? Maybe you're just scared to say yes.

Gran always says scared isn't a good enough reason to say no to something that might be good."

"Then your grandmother is a stronger person than I am."

What Nash did, helping those kids in LA, must have taken so much courage and compassion. It couldn't all be gone just because one kid betrayed him. Then again, wasn't she hiding out here in Martins Gap because of betrayal, too? "What if what you really need is to prove to yourself you still can see the good in kids like that? What's the worst that could happen?"

He shook his head and gave a dark, low laugh. "I could get shot again. And this time the kid may not miss."

"Cowboys and Indians," she said, remembering his earlier comment that now had such a different edge to it.

"Cops and robbers," he said, his features showing a hint of humor.

"Cars and knitting. It's an idea so crazy it just might work."

"It probably won't work," Nash said. "But maybe I ought to try anyway."

Allie Pleiter, an award-winning author and RITA® Award finalist, writes both fiction and nonfiction. Her passion for knitting shows up in many of her books and all over her life. Entirely too fond of French macarons and lemon meringue pie, Allie spends her days writing books and avoiding housework. Allie grew up in Connecticut, holds a BS in speech from Northwestern University and lives near Chicago, Illinois.

Visit the Author Profile page at Harlequin.com for more titles.

Coming Home to Texas

Allie Pleiter

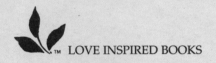 LOVE INSPIRED BOOKS

Recycling programs
for this product may
not exist in your area.

ISBN-13: 978-0-373-71947-1

Coming Home to Texas

Copyright © 2016 by Alyse Stanko Pleiter

www.Harlequin.com

Printed in U.S.A.

He has sent me to bind up the brokenhearted...
to bestow on them a crown of beauty instead of
ashes, the oil of joy instead of mourning, and a
garment of praise instead of a spirit of despair.
—*Isaiah* 61:1–3

For Amanda
For all she is becoming

Acknowledgments

Special thanks again to Beverly Brown and Donnis Baggett, the owners of the Lucky B Bison Ranch in Bryan, Texas, who continue to support me with information, hospitality and friendship. Thanks also to Ron and Theresa Miskin at the Buffalo Wool Company for explaining to me all about bison fiber.

Chapter One

Deputy sheriff Nash Larson walked up to the small red car with Georgia plates and waited for the woman to roll down her car window. "License and registration, please."

The woman gave a loud sniff as she fumbled through her handbag and glove compartment. "Sure," she gulped out in a wobbly voice. A cryer. Why did women always think crying was the way to ditch a speeding ticket?

Why? The lead weight in Nash's stomach told him it was because it *worked*. This woman was driving too fast for a rainy night in the middle of nowhere, with out-of-state plates, way too late at night, and he still felt the compulsion to be nice rather than read her the riot act, the way she probably deserved. At least she was smart enough to keep her doors locked and not roll down her window until he showed her his badge. Alone on a Texas back road at 11:45 p.m. was no time for Southern hospitality. "Do you know how fast you were going?" he inquired.

"I should have been paying attention." The lilt of her Southern drawl, combined with that thing that happened to women's voices when they cried, pulled even more reluctant sympathy from him. "I was upset," she added, as if that needed explaining.

Nash looked at the license. Ellen Buckton took a nice photo and had a pretty smile—in other words, her photo looked nothing like her current disheveled and tearful appearance. "Maybe tonight wasn't the best night to drive so late, Ms. Buckton."

"Miss," she corrected, her eyes brimming over with tears. "I'm sorry." She reached for a tissue from the nearly empty box on the seat next to her—a seat mounded with used, crumpled tissues. She'd been crying for the past hundred miles from the looks of it. "I just wanted to get home." That last word trailed off in a small sob.

The plates and license were from Georgia. "You're a long way from home, Miss Buckton. Everything okay?"

Nash wanted to whack his own forehead. *Well, that was a foolish question. The woman is far from home crying and you ask if everything's okay?*

"I just…" She pulled in shuddering breaths in an attempt to stem the tears. "I just broke off my engagement." She wiggled her naked left ring finger as Exhibit A. "I'm only about a half hour from my gran's house, where I grew up. I guess I just wanted to get there as fast as I could." She shut her eyes and held out her hand while visibly bracing herself, as if whatever ticket he was about to give her would sting. "Go ahead. I deserve it. It's not like you'd be ruining a lovely day or anything."

Nash had never been the kind of man who could kick a soul when they were down. People were supposed to be friendly in Texas, right? That was part of the reason he'd left LA—that, and the two bullet holes in his shoulder and thigh. Being hunted down tended to make a man rethink his zip code. And yearn to play nice, at least once in a while.

"I'm sorry for your troubles. But driving 80 in a 65 zone won't make anything better. I expect you already knew that."

She looked up at him with wet, wide eyes. They were a brilliant light blue—like pool water or a turquoise gemstone—something her license photo hadn't captured in the slightest. "I should have been more careful." She sighed. "I should have been a lot of things."

He couldn't bring himself to give her a ticket. Not when he had the chance to make her day just a bit less horrible. Instead, he decided tonight was his chance to show Ellen Buckton that not every man on planet Earth was a heartless creep. Nash handed back her license and paperwork, bringing the most tender, astonished look to her face. "Will you be more careful for the rest of your drive?"

She nodded like a schoolchild. "Oh, yes, absolutely. I promise."

"You know where you're going?"

"Like the back of my hand." She wiped her eyes. "Although that's no excuse for speeding, Officer. I know that. But I grew up around here, and I could find my way home with my eyes closed—not that I'm going to, of course." Now that he'd "pardoned" her, the words were tumbling out in grateful puddles. "I'll be extra careful, and I'm only about thirty minutes away." She fumbled under the pile of tissues to produce a large ziplock bag filled with dark oblong objects. "Do you like biscotti, Officer—" she peered at his name tag "—Larson?"

Cookies? "Um, I do, but you can understand why it might not be such a smart idea for me to be accepting goodies from you."

Her eyes went wide again. "I've eaten a dozen already, so I really do need to get them out of the car. But you're right. I mean, I didn't mean to imply you could be bribed with cookies or anything, because I'm sure you can't. And I wouldn't. It was just a thank-you for being so nice and all."

She was babbling, and he could tell that she knew it. Poor thing. She really needed just to get wherever she was going and put herself to bed. "Drive safe, Miss Buckton, and stay under the speed limit." Then, for reasons he couldn't explain, he added, "And, for what it's worth, I'm sorry about your engagement."

He was worried that would start the waterworks again, but instead it brought the strangest look to her face. "You know, you're the first person to say 'I'm sorry' to me about this whole thing. Kind of tells you something, doesn't it?"

Nash wasn't quite sure if he was supposed to answer that question. Instead he tipped his hat in a way that felt absurdly nouveau-Texan and said, "Good night."

"Good night, Officer Larson. And thank you. You're the first nice thing that's happened to me today."

Well, thought Nash as he walked back to his cruiser. *Cookies and compliments. Maybe Texas won't be so bad after all.*

Funny how a life can blow up in an instant.

Ellie Buckton looked out the kitchen window and stared at the pastures that made up the Blue Thorn Ranch. She'd grown up in this house, Gran's home, the Buckton family homestead, where her oldest brother's new family now lived. The place where her parents had lived until her mother died when Ellie was thirteen, and where Daddy had bravely held down the fort until his own death three years ago. These walls held so much— almost too much—history. But for now, this would be the place where she hid until she could figure out what to do next.

Almost everything about the place felt the same. That stuck-in-time atmosphere was partly why it had been years since Ellie had felt any yearning to come back here. Then again, she couldn't remember ever not knowing what to do next.

She heard Gran's slippered feet shuffle into the kitchen. As she turned to meet those wise turquoise eyes, Ellie's chest filled with warmth instead of the tightrope tension that had lived there since her heartbreaking discovery three days ago.

"How are you, sweetheart?" Gran stood beside her, leaning her white-tufted head on Ellie's shoulder. Gran always smelled of lavender soap and peace. The familiar scents reminded Ellie why she had run here. "Better?"

She wasn't, really. Still, relief at being anywhere but Atlanta might be classified as "better."

"In a way," Ellie sighed in reply. "I don't think 'better' is on the menu for a while yet."

Gran sighed, too. In her eighty-five years, she'd known her share of heartbreak and hard times, as well. "A broken heart is a hard fence to jump. And you had yours broke but good." She gave Ellie a hug. "I meant what I said yesterday—you stay here as long as you like." Her eyes grew sharp, her frown sour. "That Derek fellow is a low-down swine for cheating on you the way he did." She placed her thin hand over Ellie's own. "But coming home was the right thing to do. I'm glad you're here for however long I've got you. I plan to pamper you eight ways to Sunday, and then some more on top of that."

Derek.

Her now ex-fiancé had left three text messages and two voice mails on her phone since Tuesday. Ellie had deleted all of them without reading or listening.

Gran put the kettle on the burner while Ellie took a long sip of coffee. "I've been meaning to ask you," Gran said as she reached for the little china canister that held all her tea bags. "Did you keep the ring after you found that good-for-nothing chef cozying up to your best friend? Or did you give it back?"

Ellie managed a smile. "Actually, I thought about putting it in the blender. But I like my blender too much."

Gran raised a gray eyebrow. "I've got a meat grinder in here somewhere. We could mangle it but good, take photos with that snazzy phone of yours and email them to him."

Ellie loved that her grandmother had embraced the digital age, even if the old woman did crash her computer twice a week and still hadn't quite mastered the intricacies of texting. Gran had sent her a "come home" email practically every hour since St. Patrick's Day night when Ellie found her fiancé planting passionate kisses on her best friend and would-have-been maid of honor, Katie.

Derek and Katie. She still couldn't get the sight of them with their arms wrapped around each other out of her head. She'd discovered the pair necking like teenagers in the pantry of the restaurant where they were all working on a company-wide St. Patrick's Day event. Having an engagement destroyed was one thing, but having it self-destruct in front of her boss and most of her friends was a new level of torture. Going back to work when her leave of absence was over would be no picnic.

"No thanks, Gran." Ellie sat down at the table, feeling tired despite the early hour. She hadn't slept especially well last night, despite the exhaustion she'd felt after hoisting two suitcases into the trunk of her car and driving the fourteen hours to Blue Thorn Ranch. "I don't want to send Derek anything at all, not even hate mail."

"I hope they yank his television spot when they find out what he did to you." With a warm curl of delight, Ellie realized Gran was getting out the makings for pancakes. Gran's pancakes were the cure for just about every hurt life had to offer, and Ellie hadn't tasted them in months. Today she wanted them more than anything.

"I wouldn't be surprised if an escapade like that made him even more popular," Ellie admitted as she reached into the cabinet behind her to hand Gran the flour. "He'd use it, too, if I know him. Derek loves getting attention from the press, even if it's negative, and the whole bad-boy-chef persona is hot right now."

Gran held up a spatula like a battle sword. "Not with me, it ain't." Adele Buckton was no one to mess with.

Ellie loved the "nobody hurts my grandbaby" glare in Gran's eyes. After losing her best friend and fiancé in one heartbreaking revelation, it bothered her immensely that no one she'd told in Atlanta had seemed surprised that Derek would cheat on her. And very few seemed ready to rise to her defense. Had no one really expected them to work out? Had everyone hid their doubts or, worse yet, their suspicions as to Derek's ability to be faithful? "I guess the bride-to-be's always the last to know."

"It ain't fine with your brother, neither," Gran added. "Gunner would be on his way over there right now to tan his hide if it weren't for all this trouble with the herd."

Ellie's big brother, Gunner, was just the type to drive fourteen hours to pummel Derek for what he'd done. Like their grandmother, Gunner never swallowed threats or insults with any grace. Having been in her shoes—finding the love of his life in the arms of another—not too many years ago, Ellie could see how

Gunner wouldn't hesitate to make Derek pay for his infidelity.

Things were a bit different now. Gunner had found love and had married a wonderful woman, gaining a sweet young stepdaughter in the process. Even though he was the oldest, Ellie would never have guessed Gunner would marry before herself or their younger twin siblings, Luke and Tess. Married life clearly suited him, but Ellie just couldn't decide if Gunner's newlywed happiness gave her hope or rubbed salt in the wound of her own romantic failure.

"What's going on with the herd?" Blue Thorn Ranch had been reborn from her father's failing cattle operation into a thriving bison ranch thanks to Gunner, but the transition was still recent enough to produce new challenges all the time.

"We think someone's been taking potshots at our animals," Gran explained as she poured the tea into the pot to steep and then flicked a spray of water onto the griddle. It sizzled and popped, indicating the griddle was hot and ready for pancake batter. "The herd is edgy, and we've heard rifles at night. Gunner has a meeting with the sheriff's office this morning to coordinate the investigation."

Ellie's ears picked up on the sound of little feet galloping down the stairs. "Pancake Saturday!" little Audie cried as she burst into the room clad in bright pink pajamas. The girl stopped in front of Ellie. "Aunt Ellie? When did you get here?" Ellie found her waist encircled in pink arms that squeezed deliciously tight.

"Long after your bedtime, Audie. How's my favorite niece liking the fourth grade?"

Audie looked up at Ellie, making a face. "Fractions are awful, but I love science and art. Gunnerdad says math is useful, but I mostly think it's complicated and boring."

Gunnerdad. Audie's invented Gunner-and-Dad combination never failed to put a smile on Ellie's face. He made a big show out of tolerating the name, but the way that man looked at his stepdaughter told everyone how much he loved his new role as Audie's "Gunnerdad."

"Where's your mother?" Gran asked the girl as she handed plates to Ellie to set the breakfast table.

Audie replied by squinting her eyes shut and sticking out her tongue.

"Sick again?" Gran asked. "I'd guess you're getting a baby brother, then. Only baby boys give their mamas that much trouble."

Gunner was going to be a father. And despite the morning sickness, Ellie knew how thrilled the loving couple was about their upcoming arrival. How smart an idea was it to run away to a house so full of happiness? Ellie's coffee turned bitter in her mouth, as if her own life soured all the more by comparison.

Just as the pancakes were dished up, Gunner walked in from the barn. Ellie had seen him last night when she'd arrived, but in the light of day, he looked so different from the rebellious big brother she'd once known. Here was a "bad boy" who'd grown into a fine, upstanding—but admittedly still stubborn—man. The kind of man she'd once thought Derek was becoming. Evidently some bad boys never outgrew their bad. "Hi, Els," he said, giving her an extra-tight hug before sitting down at the table. Ellie reeled with a sudden and deep gratitude to feel her big brother by her side. Sure, all the love-and-marriage happiness in this house stung a bit—a lot, actually—but Gran was right; this was the best place to hide and heal.

At least that was what she hoped.

"Don's bringing out the new deputy when he comes today," Gunner said as he accepted a large helping of pancakes. "This guy's from California. He's worked with vandalism cases."

"Vandalism?" Ellie questioned. "Is someone spray-painting graffiti on your bison?"

Audie giggled.

"Do you remember that internet video I sent you, Audie? The one with the Irish sheepherder who dyes his flock colors like Easter eggs every spring?" Ever since she'd met her new niece, Ellie had snuck in time to amuse the little girl with videos and playful messages as a break from her day job of amusing food critics and reporters as a public relations specialist for Atlanta's largest chain of restaurants.

Audie nodded and she turned to her stepdad. "Can we do that? Dye the bison? Maybe just the babies? We could make a video just like the shepherd man!"

Gunner shot Ellie a "thanks for nothing" look before issuing a declarative "No, we can't." For a new dad, Gunner had the authoritative father tone down pat. It shouldn't surprise her—their father had been a master of such tones, but never with the touch of amusement and affection that softened Gunner's words.

"But Ellie told me you can make yarn out of bison fur the same way you make it out of sheep fur, so why can't we?"

"That's true," Ellie said, smiling at Gunner. She and Audie had been emailing fun facts to each other for months now, and evidently her new niece had been paying attention. "I can see it now—the blue bison of Blue Thorn Ranch."

Gunner's frown predicted a few words for his little sister after breakfast. "I run a ranch, not a circus," he growled, digging into his pancakes.

Ellie winked at her niece. Yes, this was a good place to run and hide after all.

Chapter Two

"*Oh*, give me a home, where the buffalo roam…'"

Nash turned to look at his boss, County Sheriff Don Mellows. "You gotta be kidding me."

Don stopped his singing and chuckled. "I am. No deer and antelope playing here. These here are American bison, anyways, so don't you be calling them *buffalo* in front of Gunner Buckton."

Buckton? Wasn't that the name from the traffic stop last night? "Bison not *buffalo*—got it." The leap from LAPD to this local County Sheriff Department seemed to grow longer and wider with each new day.

And stranger. Nash was still getting accustomed to his deputy position in this small town and its rural surroundings. Don was about as down-home cowboy as anyone Nash had ever seen, right down to the boots and *y'alls*. For a city cop used to dealing with gangs and criminals, this was new territory.

"Why are we here again?"

"Buckton thinks someone may be taking shots at his

animals." Don pulled up to the ranch's large entrance gate. Nash tried to calculate the distance from this place to where he'd stopped Ellen Buckton last night—the geography just about fit. "He's worried there may be some foul play involved," Don continued. "I figured your background might be useful while we take a look-see."

"Has Buckton got enemies?" Nash surveyed the rolling pasture, spying a few of the large brown animals milling about. Tall green grass, wide blue sky, livestock roaming—the whole thing looked like something out of a travel brochure. If this was the home Ellen was running to, Nash had to agree it looked like a good, big place to hide. After all, the sprawling space of the region had drawn him for much the reason.

"Enemies? He's got 'em. Most men do. The family's been around for ages—everybody knows the Bucktons— but they got in a row with a big real estate developer last year. Could be someone's not too happy about the spiffy condo development that got stalled on account of it. Of course, could be just stupid kids. Not likely rustlers, though—they would've taken the animals, not tried to scare 'em." Don punched the button on the gate's intercom. "Howdy, y'all. It's Don from the sheriff's office."

A far cry from standing in a Kevlar vest yelling "LAPD! Open up!" Texas really was its own world. And now—at least for now—it was Nash's, too. He looked down at his steel-toed shoes and wondered what his feet would look like in fancy cowboy boots like Don wore. Or whether Don's wide hat would suit him. He couldn't mesh the images in his mind. Did you *have* to be a cowboy if you lived in Texas? Austin was a world-class metropolitan city, admittedly a bit of a quirky one, but parts of LA were downright strange, so that was no clue.

"Well, hello there, Don," a female voice drawled over the crackly intercom speaker. "Gunner's in the barn, so pull right on up. I'll put some coffee on for afterward. And there's blueberry pie."

Don smiled. "Blueberry pie. Miss Adele, you do know how to make a man's day." Don waggled an eyebrow at Nash. "That'd be Miss Adele, Gunner's grandma. Was a time she and her husband ran this place." Then he added, "Anybody ever feed you pie back in California?"

Nash thought about the offer of cookies late last night. This had to be the place. If he saw Ellen Buckton, this morning would get a whole lot more interesting. "No."

"Well, then, you ought to be glad you're in Texas, Larson. A sheriff eats good in Martins Gap."

The gate rolled open to let the cruiser head up the curving lane. The gravel road bent through the tall grasses to end at a cluster of buildings. Large low barns surrounded a sprawling stone ranch house with a wide front porch. A sizable fenced-in corral off one barn held a pair of bison, one large, one smaller. "Nice folks, the Bucktons," Don went on. "Been on this land for ages. Miss Adele's husband and son raised cattle. Gunner Jr.—that's who you'll meet today—turned the operation over to bison a few years back, right after his dad died. Good people." Don turned to Nash. "But even good people can collect some bad enemies, ain't that the truth."

"It is." Nash could easily agree, having been a good cop who had made nasty enemies by putting away a gang lord or two in LA. After several months on high alert as the top target of two gang hit lists, his rehabilitation for a pair of close-call gunshot wounds had been enough to make him want to get out of that city. A friend had passed along the opening here in the sheriff's department, and Nash had felt as if God had opened up the escape hatch for which he'd been praying.

As they got out of the cruiser, an elderly woman with a cane made her way down the porch steps. The resemblance was enough to confirm Nash's guess—this was where Ellen had been heading.

Don smiled and waved. "One of these days we've got to meet up for *good* reasons, Miss Adele."

"I hear you, Don. Let's have you and Linda out for dinner one of these days." Miss Adele raised a gray eyebrow at Nash. "So this is your new deputy?"

"Nash Larson," Don introduced. "Brought him on all the way from California last month."

She walked over, extending a friendly hand. "Nice to finally meet you, Nash. Welcome to Martins Gap. How are you liking it so far?"

The screen door opened behind Miss Adele and out walked Ellen Buckton, eyes startled wide and mouth open. "It's you."

She was much prettier in the daylight—in fact, she looked almost nothing like the tearful mess of a woman who'd offered him biscotti last night. "Good afternoon, Miss Buckton. Glad to see you made it safe and sound."

Don looked at Nash while Miss Adele looked at her granddaughter. Nash kept silent—the explanation ought to be Ellen's territory, given the circumstances.

"Ellie?" Miss Adele clearly wasn't going to wait.

Ellie. That suited her much more than Ellen, Nash thought. Her tawny blond hair—pulled up into a mess on the top of her head last night—hung in loose curves over her shoulders. The eyes—remarkably blue last night—were breathtaking in the full light of day.

Only right now they looked mortified. "Um…well…" She thrust her hands into the back pockets of her jeans and shifted her weight. "I got pulled over for speeding last night, Gran. I guess I was in too much of a hurry to get here."

Don shot Nash a surprised look. Nash hadn't entered the stop in his official records. He just shrugged, unsure what he was supposed to do or say.

Miss Adele moved over to wrap an arm around Ellie. "Of course you were, sweetheart, but a speeding ticket? Really?"

"No ticket, ma'am," Nash offered. "I could see how upset she was, so I just let her off with a warning and her promise to take it slower the rest of the way here."

"Thanks for that again, really," Ellie offered with a small smile. "You were the only good spot in a horrible day."

That set a small glow in Nash's stomach. Law enforcement didn't offer a man a lot of reasons to be the *good* part of someone's day—more often just the opposite. A large part of him hoped that balance would change out here. "Glad to help."

"Well—" Don pulled a notebook from his shirt pocket "—now that we're all friendly like, how about you tell me what's been going on?"

"Here comes my brother now," Ellie said, nodding at a tall man with the same tawny hair walking toward them, wiping his hands on a bright blue bandanna. "He can fill you in better than Gran or I."

Nash and Don spent the next half hour listening to Gunner Buckton's account of finding fences messed with, hearing rifle fire near the animals and the general edginess of the herd.

"Any idea why someone would want to scare or harm your herd?" Nash asked as Gunner showed photographs he'd printed from his smartphone of clipped fence wires.

"That's what has me stumped, frankly." Gunner pushed his hat back on his head, revealing the brilliant blue eyes Nash had now realized were a family trait. "Bison aren't people-friendly. And an agitated cow or bull can be downright dangerous. Whoever's doing this is really brave, really quick or just too stupid to recognize the danger."

"Kids," Don pronounced. Nash had to admit, it made the most sense. Anyone wanting to truly hurt the Bucktons could pick a dozen safer ways to do damage. Still, bragging rights for trying to nick or free a bison sounded like a pretty far-fetched stunt, even for kids.

"They'll be hurt or worse if this keeps up. It's making the herd anxious. We're just coming into calving season. I've got my hands full as it is."

"We'll do our best to find the ones responsible, Gunner." Don clasped the rancher on the shoulder. "I'll have a chat with a few of the likely suspects and see if I can dig anything up. Hopefully, this'll all die down on its own soon enough. Now how 'bout that pie your gran was offering? I want to show Nash here what down-home cooking really tastes like."

"Thanks again. For last night, I mean," Ellie offered as she refilled Nash Larson's coffee cup. They were standing by the coffeemaker while Sheriff Don, Gunner and Gran sat around the kitchen table. "I meant what I said about you being the only nice thing that happened that day." Not to mention the nicest thing she'd had to look at in nearly a thousand miles. He had brownish-red hair with a ruddy coloring that would have made him look boyish were it not for the severe features that made up his face. She got the impression he was a tough guy squelching a soft edge—or a caring man who'd had the tough shell forced upon him. Given his profession, it could easily be either.

"You really drove all the way here from Atlanta in one day?"

"Yeah, well, that's how badly I wanted to get out of town. After my little…discovery…I stumbled around for the rest of the week claiming 'sick days,' but by Friday I knew I didn't want to spend another hour listening to my friends whisper about how my fiancé had gotten caught snuggled up against the croutons with someone I *thought* was my best friend." Ellie shrugged off the lingering sting of that statement. "Two emails, three suitcases and a triple-shot latte later, I was on the road."

Nash raised an eyebrow. "Croutons?"

"Derek is a chef. Katie works for the same restaurant chain I do—did. I'm not entirely sure I'll want the job waiting for me when I go back. The big breakup was alarmingly…public at a St. Patrick's Day event involving the whole company."

"Ouch. And no one could muster up an 'I'm sorry'?"

He'd remembered what she'd said last night. That stuck somewhere deep—she'd felt so dismissed and invisible since that whole drama. How she could feel so overlooked after such a public scene still stumped her.

"The St. Patrick's Day Fest is a big event involving all our restaurants, so there were rushing people and chaos and even cameras everywhere—Derek is a bit of a celebrity. Thankfully, there weren't any cameras nearby at that particular moment. I would have thought he was swamped with work—he certainly didn't seem to have time for me that day—but clearly he had time for…other people. When I confronted him, he just sort of shut down into chef mode, shouting about food details and telling me there just wasn't time for personal drama."

Nash's jaw worked. It was gratifying to see a perfect stranger horrified by Derek's behavior—proof she wasn't some oversensitive victim. "No time? Really? I hope you gave it to him anyway."

Ellie swallowed the lump in her throat, remembering the "it couldn't be helped" shrug Derek had given her as he wiped the last of Katie's lipstick from his chin.

The lack of shock or even regret stung worst of all. How could she have so blind to the growing indifference Derek had been showing her? She'd put his distance down to stress, but his cooling toward her had been only because Derek was heating it up with her so-called best friend. Who knew "lukewarm" could burn so much?

"I told him—" she didn't bite back the bitter edge she gave the words "—that if he had time to cheat on me with my best friend, he could make the time to man up and apologize for it."

Nash took a swallow of coffee and nodded. "I wouldn't have been half that kind."

"Thanks." She meant it. Ellie needed people to take her side. The number of people at GoodEats who had looked at her with a sad sort of "didn't you see this coming?" expression was one of the reasons she'd packed her car and fled to the ranch.

"What are you going to do now?"

She didn't have a real answer. "Eat. Bake. Knit. Restore my faith in human nature. Maybe make yarn."

"Knit?"

"It's what I do to calm down or feel…" She reached for a way to explain what the steady click of the needles over the yarn did for her soul. "Oh, I don't know, comfort, I suppose? I don't cook—not well, not like Derek or Katie—so I express my creativity with yarn." She looked out the window over the kitchen sink. "You can make really good yarn from bison hair, you know. We've never done it here, but I've always wanted to try it."

Nash seemed to have caught her hesitant tone. "But?"

"But I'm pretty sure Gunner finds the idea far-fetched. Not the artistic type, my brother. But he has a good head for business, so if I make a practical case for it..." She ran her hands through her hair, wondering if she was boring the guy with her oddball ideas. "It's just a dumb idea I had. I don't know if it will go anywhere, but it will give me something to do until I figure out what's next."

"How long are you staying?"

"Gran said I could stay as long as I wanted, though I'll have to go back eventually. I've got an apartment and supposedly still a job in Atlanta. If I'm smart, I'll be back before the wedding and gala season, but those months can be brutal in the restaurant business. I'm not sure I've got the strength for brutal left in me, if you know what I mean."

Nash frowned at her strangely, as if the choice of words had touched a raw nerve. "Yeah, believe it or not, I do know."

She wasn't sure it was safe to ask. "How?"

A flash shot through his moss-green eyes. "Let's just say LA specializes in brutal, and I was done with it, too."

"Are you hoping here will be less brutal? I'm pretty sure you'll get your wish as long as you stay outside of Austin. Martins Gap can come close to boring."

He managed a slip of a smile. "Nobody calls the sheriff out because they're bored."

She felt a smile—the first in what felt like ages—turn up the corners of her lips as she sipped her coffee. "Oh, I guess that's true. Bison Crimes Unit, huh?"

Now he genuinely laughed. "It's a far cry from vice and vandalism, I'll give you that. Gang members can be big, but they don't come in thousand-pound hairy versions with big horns. At least not yet."

Ellie returned her gaze to the pastures. Blue Thorn Ranch had seen its share of challenges over the years, but it was hard to imagine anyone seeking to do the family or its animals harm, even for a thrill. "Why would someone want to harm the herd?"

"Maybe they're not trying to harm the herd. Maybe they're just proving something to buddies. For a thrill or a dare. To join some gangs in LA, you had to shoot someone. It didn't matter who, just that you shot to kill."

Ellie felt the same distaste that drew his jaw tight. "That's awful. We don't have gangs out here."

Nash shrugged. "Maybe not like in LA or even Atlanta or Austin, but kids anywhere will try to prove their worth in bad ways if no one shows them their worth in good ways."

It should have made it better—to consider the attacks might not be deliberate and personal—but it still sent a shudder down Ellie's spine. "But to an animal? It's cruel. And even if you forget the compassion part—it's frightening when a big, dangerous animal could turn around and kill you."

"All the more reason to think it's kids who aren't thinking through the consequences, wouldn't you say?"

Ellie wrapped her hands around the coffee mug, suddenly craving its warmth. "I don't know." She caught Nash's eyes. "I didn't know I was coming home to an episode of cops and robbers."

He grinned ever so slightly. "That's okay. I didn't know I was moving here to an episode of cowboys and Indians."

"Then I guess we're both in for a surprise."

Chapter Three

"That's one of them foreign sports cars, isn't it?"

Nash looked up from under the hood of his 1980 Datsun 280ZX to find Theo Kennedy, the local pastor, standing in his garage doorway. Kennedy was twice Nash's age—graying at the temples and a bit thick around the middle—but he was a likable guy, and it was clear people in town loved him dearly.

Nash had been to church once or twice since coming to town, liked the local congregation, but hadn't realized he'd drawn enough attention to warrant a pastoral visit. Evidently what Don kept telling him about small towns like Martins Gap was true—nothing ever truly went unnoticed.

"It's an import, yes. Japanese, to be exact." Nash wiped his palms on a nearby towel and offered a hand to the pastor.

"Don't see too many of those around here. Looks fast," the man said, peering at the array of tubes and parts under the vehicle's long, sleek hood.

It was true. Nash had seen nothing but domestic cars in his travels around the small town. He'd also noticed his share of glares that clearly translated to "Why ain't you drivin' an American car?" when he'd taken the Z out for drives. Some days the stares didn't bother him. Other days they made him feel about as foreign and shunned as the import. "She is fast. When she runs right, that is. She threw a fan belt on the highway two days ago and is currently giving me a hard time."

"We got a hardware store and a garage in town. Both of them carry car parts."

Nash laughed. "Not these. This little lady has very exclusive taste in accessories. I didn't bring all my spare parts in the move from LA, and now I'm regretting it." At least the Z was reasonable compared to other foreign cars. Some of the Italian models could cost his yearly salary in parts and labor, but the Z sucked up only a slightly painful portion of his spare cash. "Still," he continued as he dropped the hood down and heard it latch with a satisfying *click*, "I don't mind tinkering with a few things while I wait for parts to ship."

"Like to get grease under your fingernails, do you?" Pastor Kennedy asked.

"It's a good stress release from law enforcement. And a nice change to be making things run instead of stepping in when they don't." Nash moved his toolbox from one of the two metal stools beside his workbench and motioned for the pastor to sit down. "Something I can do for you, Pastor Kennedy?" As soon as the words left his mouth, Nash realized that was probably a dangerous thing to ask a pastor. Yes, he ought to get better connected in the community, but he didn't exactly feel ready to set down roots or open himself up to relationships.

"Please, just Theo or Pastor Theo if you like, since I am here on church business. There is something I'm hoping you might help with." The man picked up an air filter from Nash's workbench and examined it. "Don told me you worked with at-risk youth in LA. I think we have some trouble brewing with ours."

Nash's stomach tightened. He'd always found "at risk" a sanitized and clinical term for hoodlums and gangbangers who seemed closer to savages than humans some days. He often could glimpse the person hiding under the animal, and he knew the value of that sight. But what he'd told Ellie was true; he wasn't ready to go back to that kind of brutal. He returned a wrench to its place in the toolbox rather than respond.

"Don also tells me you agree with him that whoever's making trouble over at the Blue Thorn is most likely young folk," Theo went on.

Nash sat down opposite the man. "Seems like it, yes. Only it's too early to say for sure."

"Kids need something good to do, or they find something not-so-good to do, don't you think?"

Nash tried to calculate polite ways out of this conversation, regretting that he'd sat down. "That's been my experience."

Theo shifted on the stool. "Our boys need something good to do. Something new and interesting."

The pastor was staring at the car. It wasn't hard to see where this was heading. Nash snapped the lid of the toolbox closed with what he hoped was finality. "There's always auto shop at the high school."

Theo chuckled. "If you met Clive Tyler, you'd know why I might be lookin' for someone with a bit more... appeal."

Nash remembered Mr. Smith, the bug-eyed, odd little man who'd been his own auto-shop teacher in high school. "Smitty" was as uncool as could be and no one Nash had ever wanted to spend his free time with at that age. "I guarantee you, a deputy has probably just as little appeal to boys that age."

"Well, a sheriff like Don, maybe. But you're different. They'd take to you."

They do take to me. And I take to them. And then they shoot me and I end up in Texas. "Not so much, Pastor."

"Don't sell yourself short. Our boys who play sports—they've got places to go and coaches looking after them. The boys who don't, well, I feel like they're falling through the cracks."

"It happens." How like a pastor to find and hit Nash's soft spot: kids who fell through the cracks. Kids who didn't fit the mold, who either didn't stand out or stood out in all the wrong ways. *A knack is not an obligation. I moved here to get away from all that.*

"The thing is, Nash, I want to start an after-school program for them at the church. Someplace positive for them to go. Something constructive for them to do, even if only for one day a week. I need something that catches their interest. Something like that car over there."

To Kennedy's credit and Nash's growing regret, the

pastor was dead-on in his thinking. To a high school boy, was there anything more attractive—other than a high school girl—than a cool car? A year ago Nash would have jumped at this opportunity. Building relationships with the local teens was always a good idea in law enforcement. It was just that the past six months had trampled Nash's desire to do anything with teens, at least for now.

Nash wiped his hands down his face. "Look, Theo, your idea's a good one, but I don't think I'm your guy."

"Why not? No one around here drives anything like this. It's a head turner of a vehicle. Are you afraid a foreign car won't—" Theo searched for the word, obviously not a man who spent time under the hood "—translate to the beat-up domestic cars they drive? Folks out here pretty much divide between Ford and Chevy and that's it."

Nash laughed. It was the most absurd version of giving a guy the benefit of the doubt he'd heard in months. "No, I know how to work on American cars. Most of it 'translates,' but I'm still not your guy."

"Why? Don told me you worked with inner-city youth for years at your last post."

Pastors must take a course in persistence at seminary. "Did he tell you why I left?"

"No."

There was no way around it now. "I left because one of those inner-city youth I worked with put two bullets in me. I'm only here now because he missed what he was aiming at and hit my shoulder and my leg. So you can see why I'm not your guy."

Theo looked down for a moment, and Nash rose off the stool to close the rest of his workbench drawers. That wasn't so bad. His gut didn't knot up at the words like it usually did.

"Actually, I still think you are the right guy," Theo said. "We got a saying around these parts about getting back up on the horse that threw you."

Nash sent him as dark a look as he dared. "That particular horse *shot* me. With intent to kill. So believe me when I tell you I'm in no hurry to mount up again, Pastor. There isn't an 'it'll do you good' version of this."

"You're what those boys need. Half the boys I want to reach have cars, and the other half are saving up for one. We have an old garage in the back of the church parking lot. It's been used for storage in the past but it's mostly empty now. I got Willie down at the garage to say he'd donate a junker for them to learn on, only Willie doesn't have the time to do the teaching. I was hoping you would help."

"What those boys need is someone who will believe in them. And right now, that isn't me."

"Don told me the sheriff's department would be in favor of anything that built connections with the local youth. He'd let you have the time to run the program and even kick in toward expenses if there are any."

Pastor Theo had done his advance work. Where was the slow drag of big-city bureaucracy when you needed it? "Don should know this isn't something I can say yes to right now."

"You don't have to agree this minute. Just say you'll think about it." Theo held out a hand for a shake.

Nash was cornered. Don was on board, Theo was standing right in front of him and Nash would look like a jerk if he turned the pastor down cold for such a worthwhile program. The best he could hope for now was to say he'd consider it and start up a search for a better candidate. He tried not to grimace when he shook the pastor's hand. "I'll give it some thought. But I don't think I'll change my mind."

"You'll forgive my saying so, but it'll be my prayer that you will. Remember, the place we least want to go is often where God brings the most fruit."

Nash gave him an "I doubt that" look as he snapped off the garage light.

Theo sighed as they walked out of the garage. "I'm glad that's settled. Now all I need to do is figure out a class for the girls and we'll be all set."

Nash's memory swung back to Ellie's description of her knitting. "I may have an idea for you there."

Ellie held up her cell-phone screen to Gran as they sat on the porch swing. "Two messages—one from Katie and one from Derek."

Gran squinted at the notifications. "What do they say?"

Ellie exhaled as she placed the phone facedown on the porch table. "I don't know. I haven't listened to them. I'm ticked that it took Katie this long to call, actually. I think this is Derek's seventh message."

Gran's eyes held a gentle reproach. "You're not going to hear what either of them has to say?"

"What is there for them to say, Gran?" Ellie felt her

chest pinch the way it did every time that painful image resurfaced. Derek and Katie had looked completely enthralled with each other. *Derek was supposed to feel that way about me*. "Part of me wants the apology he couldn't manage to choke out when I found them. Another part of me doesn't want to let him sweet talk me out of ending it." She let her head fall against Gran's shoulder. "Or worse yet, not bother even trying."

"I know it hurts bad, darlin'." Gran's arms wrapped around her—something Ellie had ached for every moment since getting her heart broken. Since she'd arrived, she'd spent hours just sitting near Gran, trying to let the pain work itself out. On the outside, she'd been sitting still staring at the pastures, but inside she'd been churning through all kinds of emotions.

Gran gave a tender laugh. "And I know it hurts extra bad because you're not knitting."

It was true. Ellie worked out most of her problems with yarn and needles. The repetitive stitches gave her time to think and process and even unwind. "Do you know what I had been knitting? A shawl for Katie to wear in the wedding. She was acting like she was my best friend. We picked out the yarn together." Ellie felt her voice catch—it seemed as if she'd cried five times a day since then. "How could she do that to me, Gran? I tell you, right now I never want to see that shawl again."

Gran shook her head. "I can't say I blame you. Seems a waste of good yarn, though. I say rip the shawl out, and enjoy doing it, but then save the yarn for something else."

Rip it out. Undo it all. Disassemble the memory and

the pain. Why not? Ellie looked up. "You know what? You're right. It's even in the back of my car." She hadn't even realized until just this moment the project had made the trip with her, sitting in the backseat of her car since before she'd decided to leave town. Suddenly dismantling the beautiful, intricate shawl seemed like the most satisfying thing she could do. "Want to help me?"

In a matter of minutes Ellie was seated back on the swing with her knitting bag and the mound of delicate sky-blue yarn that in another dozen rows would have been Katie's wedding shawl.

"Oh, honey, it's lovely," Gran cooed as she held up the nearly finished project.

It was. Ellie prided herself on the quality of her lacework—the shawl would have been stunning with the periwinkle dress she and Katie had picked out as her maid-of-honor gown. Now no one would see it. No one except Gran, that was. Ellie's heart both stung and glowed at her grandmother's praise. "Thanks for saying so. I wanted it to be special. Now it's anything but."

Gran ran her hands across the stitches. Ellie liked that Gran took time to admire the piece. It struck her just how much she needed someone to know this had been in the works. The shawl needed a witness before its demise—if so strange a thought made any sense. It felt just right when, after a few minutes, Gran handed the cloud of soft blue lace back to her and said, "Let's take this apart so it can become something new someday."

A perfect metaphor for her current life. Ellie meant it when she said, "I'm ready." She pulled the long needle from the work with a flourish, feeling weight slide off her shoulders as the stitches slid free. Finding the loose strand of yarn, she handed the ball to Gran. "I'll rip, you wind."

A tiny piece of her began to heal as she pulled the shawl apart row by row. *So you can become something new*, she told herself and the yarn. This was the wonder of Gran—she always knew just what to do to make someone feel better. Ellie couldn't yet knit with this yarn—couldn't yet create something new from such a painful memory—but she could rip out what needed to go away. She knew that tonight she would pack away the beautiful sky-blue yarn in one of Gran's trunks, and tomorrow she would start some other project. Whether or not she would listen to Katie's or Derek's phone messages would be a problem for another day.

It took almost half an hour before Ellie saw the final stitches of the big, intricate shawl disappear under her fingers. The healing relief of it unwound the knot she'd been carrying in her stomach for days. As the last stitch came undone, Ellie took what felt like her first deep breath in forever.

She'd even managed a small giggle at one of Gran's jokes when she caught sight of a sheriff's car coming up the drive.

"Well, look," Gran said. "Here comes that nice young man from the sheriff's office. Handsome fellow, don't you think?"

Ellie scowled. "After what we just did, I'd think you'd know I'm no fan of the male population right now."

Gran slid the last of the pale blue balls into Ellie's

bag. "Well, maybe I can just hope you'll be reminded that not every member of the male population is a cheating swine."

Ellie looked at Nash's tall, lean form as he got out of the car. "Nash could be just as cheating a swine as Derek, Gran. Clearly, I'm no good judge of these things. I'm off the market until further notice, and I mean it."

Gran nodded. "And you should be. You need time to heal, to sort out what happened. But that doesn't mean you can't have friends. I have no intention of you spending your entire visit cooped up in the house with me."

Ellie started to say *I have friends*, but bit back the words. In truth, she hadn't kept up with people back here in Martins Gap after moving away to business school in the big city. Her good friends from high school had taken such a different path from hers that Ellie worried they wouldn't find anything to talk about. Two of them were already married with children. She adored her new niece, Audie, liked kids and had been planning to start a family with Derek, but motherhood felt a long way off right now. Ellie settled for "I was planning to call Dottie sometime soon." It was true—as of this moment—but hadn't been a minute ago.

"I'm glad to hear it." Gran eased herself slowly up off the swing. "But right now, why don't you see to our company while I go tell Gunner the deputy's here."

Ellie stood and waved at the officer. "Nice to see you again, Deputy Larson."

He flashed her the strangest grin—almost sheepish. "Call me Nash. I'm not quite used to being called 'deputy' yet." He stepped closer. "I may have an interesting prospect for you."

"Well, now you certainly have my attention. What's up?"

"Pastor Theo came to see me yesterday."

That wasn't news. Pastor Theo was always paying calls on folks all over Martins Gap. She expected he'd show up on the ranch by the end of the week to say hello to her now that word was surely out she'd come back to the Blue Thorn. "Well, you clearly have settled in fine if Pastor Theo is paying calls on you."

"He asked me to spend some time teaching the high school boys about cars."

So Nash was a churchgoing man and a car guy. Interesting.

Nash shrugged. "I can't really help him out there." He stuffed his hands in his pockets and rested one foot on the porch stair. "But Theo was looking for someone to teach something after school to the girls."

"And?"

"And I got the idea you ought to teaching them knitting. I mean, you were talking about convincing your brother there was a market for that sort of thing, so why not create a little band of customers right here? Theo thought it was a great idea, but I promise, I didn't commit you to anything."

Sitting back in the swing, Ellie tried to decide how she felt about that. While half of her wondered where on earth he'd gotten the idea to nominate her out of the blue like that, the other half actually liked the idea. "Well." She sighed. "I suppose I owe you."

"No, you don't. You can always say no. I did."

Ellie laughed. "That's what you think. Gran calls it getting 'voluntold.' You may be the only person ever to tell Pastor Theo 'no' when he asks. And he won't stop asking."

"Well, I admit he negotiated me down to 'I'll think about it.' But no matter how long I think it over, my answer is still going to have to be no."

Ellie stood as she saw Gunner coming over from the barn. "My sister-in-law was asking me if I'd teach her how to knit booties and such for the baby. And my niece, Audie, wants to learn to make a scarf. So, believe it or not, this isn't my first request this week." She liked how the idea felt as she tried it on. "I was thinking I needed a project. But then again, so do you."

"No, I don't."

Ellie looked at him. "You need to get plugged in to this community. This seems like a pretty good way to do that. Tell you what—I'll say yes if you do, too."

His face went dark. "Then you'll be saying no. Which you shouldn't. But I won't be saying yes."

"Why? Seems like a perfectly good plan to me."

Nash scowled. "I have my reasons."

"Well, your recruitment skills leave a lot to be desired, Deputy Larson," she countered. "You can't very well tell me I ought to be saying yes when you intend to say no."

"Fine!" Nash threw up his hands and walked toward the barn. "Do whatever you want. I was just trying to help."

Doesn't sound like that to me, Ellie thought as she watched him skulk toward the barn. *What on earth was that all about?*

Chapter Four

Nash climbed out of the rugged little ATV Gunner had driven out to one of the ranch's far fences. "Big place you've got here."

"Not so much," Gunner said. "There are a lot bigger. We used to be bigger, too, but my dad hit on hard times back before he passed and had to sell off some of the land."

Nash remembered Don saying something about Gunner taking over the ranch after losing his father a few years before, and changing operations from cattle to bison. And no one had yet mentioned a mother. Had Ellie lost both parents?

Nash and Gunner began walking the fence, looking for any sign of someone being there. "Your dad raised cattle, right?"

"That's right. The bison herd was my idea." Gunner opened a gate and the two of them walked along the grass just outside the fence. "We needed something different, some way to turn the ranch back into a working operation."

"Anyone not like that idea?" Different wasn't always a welcome notion, especially in a place like this.

Gunner squatted to inspect a tamped-down clump of tall grass. "Most were curious, doubtful maybe, but nothing I'd call mean-spirited. Except for my neighbor Larkey." The rancher nodded toward the northwest side of the property, where fences marked the start of another ranch. "But that was more about real estate than livestock. He was in favor of a housing project nearby, and I got in the way by refusing to cooperate when they wanted some of my land. He did threaten one of my animals, though. We were having an argument at the time."

Nash filed that away under "useful details" in the back of his mind. "Anyone hear about it?"

Gunner gave a sour laugh. "Oh, lots of people heard about it."

"Well, it's been my experience that kids copy publicized crimes. For your sake, I hope it's only dumb kids showing off here and not someone out to harm you or your animals."

"Hey, look." Gunner rose with a sizable metal cylinder in his hand. "Rifle shell. Pretty big one at that."

Gunner had already touched it, but hopefully that wouldn't mess with ballistics. Nash reached into his pocket for an evidence bag and carefully picked it out of Gunner's palm using the bag as a glove before sealing it up. "That ought to help narrow things down." He looked up at the rancher. "I'm glad we're not picking a round out of a dead animal."

"We lose one or two a year to injury or illness before we harvest off the heard, but outside of Larkey's threats, no one's ever tried to kill one of mine. I hope no one's thinking about it now."

Nash tried to view the grassy ridge as a crime scene. It was a far cry from a Los Angeles street corner. That was certain. "How would a group of kids get out here?"

Gunner looked around. "Same as us, I suppose. ATVs, dirt bikes, maybe on horseback. This part's too far from the road to come on foot, I expect." Gunner gave him an analytical look. "You ride?"

"We did have mounted police in LA." Nash kept kicking clumps of grass aside in search of more clues. "But no, I'm a car guy."

"Like big truck or like shiny sports car?"

This was truck country, clearly. The way Gunner said *shiny* sounded as though it stood in for "fussy city car." Nash turned over a crushed can with his toe. "Am I gonna have to *git* me a truck to fit in around here?"

Gunner gave a small laugh. "Well, now, that depends. You want to fit in or stand out? My brother, Luke, never owned a truck in his life. My dad owned nothing but whatever was the biggest, fanciest truck on the market. My wife, Brooke, owned one of them bitty hatchback things when we first met, and we just bought ourselves a genuine suburban minivan seeing as we'll have two little ones soon. Fancy car might make you popular with the high school boys, now that I think of it, but then again so would a good truck."

Nash's sports car had been an asset in LA, earning him "street cred" with teens. It seemed only to earn him stares here—and not often stares of admiration. Another reason to decline Pastor Theo. "Ellie drives a hatchback, too. Anybody give her grief over it?"

Gunner laughed outright. "Well, Ellie's a city girl now. Still, it goes fast enough to earn a speeding ticket, huh?" He scratched his chin and narrowed one eye at Nash. "What made a city guy like you come all the way out here anyhow?"

"We're forty minutes from Austin, one of the fastest-developing tech centers in the country. I hardly think that qualifies as 'all the way out here.'"

Gunner spread his hands. "Look around, buddy. Martins Gap is a whole other world from Austin." The rancher fiddled with a bracket on a nearby fencepost. "One that's disappearing too fast, if you ask me."

Nash found himself again considering the easiest way to relate the chain of events that led him to Martins Gap. "I worked juvenile and street crimes in LA. Kids in gangs, vandalism, the occasional drug bust, that sort of thing. Every once in a while I'd turn a kid from a wrong choice, and each victory kept me going. I'd feel like I'd made a difference, like God was giving me a chance to put some good back in a place where most people could only see bad."

Gunner leaned against the fencepost. "That doesn't sound like a reason to leave."

"It isn't. But then one of those kids—one of the ones I thought I'd helped the most, actually—he turned on me. Went back to everything I thought he'd left behind.

By the time I found him, he was in even deeper than he'd been before."

"But you found him?"

Nash swallowed. He still hadn't found an easy way to talk about that night. "More like he found me first. Hunted me down, actually. I ended up with two bullet holes that seemed to puncture all my faith in the good I used to be able to see. I knew it was time to leave."

"It's not perfect here, but I'd like to think we've got more good than an LA street." Gunner looked out over the land, and Nash could watch the determination straighten the man's shoulders. People liked LA, but people *loved* this land in a way he hadn't thought possible. As if the grass and hills were an inseparable part of them, connected and deep-rooted. After all, Ellie had made a life in Atlanta, but she'd rushed back here at top speed when that life fell apart, certain she'd find sanctuary. He'd never had that kind of home, but he understood the appeal.

"What about Ellie's fiancé? Did you think he was a good man before all this business?"

"Derek?" Gunner returned to looking through the grass. "Only met him once, at my wedding. He's famous— one of them television-show chefs or something. I thought he was kind of full of himself, but I figured that just went with the territory." He looked up at Nash. "If I ever do get the chance to see him again, I'd like to punch his lights out for cheating on my baby sister."

He said it with such a twang that it sounded like something out of a cowboy movie, but Nash could appreciate the sentiment. Anyone who had seen the tearful hurt in Ellie's eyes would want to sock the guy who'd done that to her. "Good riddance, I suppose."

"Yes, sir. And it's nice to have her back on the ranch, even though I know it's not for keeps. She'll fiddle around here for a while, maybe get a start on that cockamamy bison-yarn idea, but soon enough it'll peter out. She'll get tired of Martins Gap and head on back to Atlanta. Ellie grew up here, but she doesn't belong in this life. She's fast-paced. Always needs to be busy, always needs a project. Organizing her wedding was the biggest project of them all, you know? She'll be fine once she finds something to replace it."

"So you think the yarn thing is just a distraction?"

"Oh, she doesn't think so, I know. But you've got to know Ellie. She's only home to lick her wounds. I'm happy to have her—don't get me wrong—but I'm not too worried we'll be adding scarves and mittens to our inventory of bison burgers and steaks."

Half of Nash was glad Ellie was a temporary resident of Martins Gap. He liked her. He'd liked her that first night they met, and while he hated to admit it, the idea of working with her on Pastor Theo's high school project appealed to him. And that was a problem, because women on the rebound were vulnerable and impulsive. One of his many botched LA relationships had been a heartbroken woman, and it had ended in a very messy way. The last thing Ellie Buckton needed was more mess. Besides, part of this relocation had been a promise to God to steer clear of emotional entanglements until he got his head on straight.

Nash wasn't in the habit of breaking promises to

God, nor did he want to give Gunner Buckton any reason to punch his lights out. Ellie Buckton could be a friend, maybe a teaching partner, but Nash would be wise to make sure it came to nothing more.

"So you'll do it, then?"

Be careful what you pray for. The words rang true in Ellie's head as she caught the enthusiasm in Pastor Theo's eyes as they sat on the ranch front porch talking about the program. How had she become old enough to mentor high schoolers? *The same way you got old enough to get married*, her heart reminded her. *Or almost get married.*

"Sure, I will. It will be fun." She meant that—mostly. She taught people to knit all the time in Atlanta, eagerly sharing her favorite pastime with anyone who showed an interest. Restaurant people were creative folks and often glommed on to crafty pursuits for their downtime. She'd spent many lunch hours—when the hectic setting permitted them to take a lunch break—on the deck behind the GoodEats offices above Derek's restaurant knitting and laughing with the corporate and food service staff.

Ellie looked around to make sure Gunner wasn't close enough to overhear. "Pastor Theo, I'd like to impose one condition, if that's okay with you."

The pastor smiled. "I can't imagine I'd say no to any request you make."

She really did like this guy, especially after all the restaurant's oversize egos. "In addition to learning knitting, I'd like the girls help me with an effort to make bison yarn from the Blue Thorn animals. Maybe they can even end up spinning their own hanks. Is that okay?"

"Bison yarn?" Pastor Theo asked. "There is such a thing?"

And there would be the Blue Thorn Fibers' first marketing challenge—most people didn't even know bison yarn existed, much less all the excellent properties of the fiber. She scooted her chair closer to the pastor's. "You can make a marvelous yarn from a bison's undercoat. It's very strong, warm and lightweight— much more so than sheep's wool. I've been dying to give it a try on the ranch, but it'll take more than just me to get it launched, and I think you've just handed me the perfect opportunity to get some help."

Now Gunner would have no reason to refuse. He'd never put up any resistance to helping church kids, and she wouldn't be taking any time from the ranch's working hands to collect the fibers. It all fit together. The welcome buzzing in the pit of her stomach dispelled the fear that had hung over her the past few days—a fear she wouldn't feel excited about anything again. That was silly, of course—she was only twenty-five and life was far from over—but the bombed-out feeling she'd carried around since finding Derek with Katie was finally starting to disappear.

"Well, then, this is starting to feel like a win-win for everybody." Pastor Theo looked up to see the ATV carrying Gunner and Nash pull up next to the barn. "Now we just have to ask God to work on Nash so that he'll do the boys' car class. I feel like God is pulling a plan together."

Was that what God was doing? It was a welcome thought for someone whose life felt as though it had been blown apart. Ellie wasn't ready to embrace her broken engagement as part of God's perfect plan— everything hurt too much for that just yet—but Pastor Theo was right. She'd see the whole of things someday, even if she couldn't see it yet. Her life was just like Katie's shawl—taken apart to become something new— and like Katie's shawl yarn, it had to lie in wait for whatever it was going to be next.

"So did she say yes?" Nash asked Pastor Theo as he walked up to the porch. He caught Ellie's eye. "She's perfect for the job."

Theo looked between Nash and Ellie. "I'd say the same of you. How do you two know each other exactly?"

Ellie gulped, not eager to recount her close call with a speeding ticket to the local pastor.

"With all due respect, Pastor, we'll have to agree to disagree about that job. As for Ellie, we met on the ranch the other day," Nash said, flashing her a quick look. Ellie made a mental note to figure out what was behind Nash's bristling refusal to help Pastor Theo. Right after she whipped the deputy up some more biscotti—or maybe a nice warm scarf—to thank him for covering for her yet again.

Pastor Theo rose. "I'm excited. And once you give in, Nash, I think you two will make a perfect team for the after-school program."

Gunner had come up onto the porch. "Nash is teaching at church? Really?"

"No, not really," Nash replied with growing exasperation. "But Ellie is."

"What are *you* teaching?" Gunner asked with a disbelieving look that irked Ellie to no end. She was perfectly capable of mentoring girls. She had the same skills and intellect she'd had before she'd yanked Derek's ring off her finger. She smiled, now more than ready to prove it. "Knitting, of course."

"Well, that's nice." Gunner's lack of interest stuck in her craw. Time to up the stakes.

"With Blue Thorn bison yarn that the girls are going to help make." She watched her brother's eyebrow rise. "Crafts and community awareness all in one. I know how you're all about community awareness, Gunner."

Gunner narrowed his eyes. "So they keep telling me." He turned toward the barn. "Nash, you've got all you need? I've got some things to check on in the barn." He threw Ellie one last dark look. "We'll talk more about this later, Els."

Ellie couldn't stifle a victorious grin. "I'm sure we will, brother dear. I've got all kinds of plans."

"You always do," Gunner called, not looking back.

Pastor Theo said his goodbyes, but Nash stared at the barn. "Why do I get the feeling I just saw the opening salvo in a sibling war?"

Ellie laughed. "Oh, not open combat. More like high-level negotiations. Gunner thinks my idea to have Blue Thorn produce bison yarn is silly. You and Pastor

Theo just handed me the perfect way to convince him otherwise."

Nash looked bemused. "I'm going to regret this, aren't I?"

"Oh, I wouldn't say that. Only, you might have to duck now and then to stay out of the line of fire." She'd thought it a witty remark, but Nash's face changed completely—and not in a good way. "Bad joke to make to a deputy?"

"Just this deputy." The tone of his voice tightened up.

Ellie came up to stand beside him. She wanted to smooth over whatever had just happened, but wasn't exactly sure how. "Have you…have you been shot? Is that it? Is that why you won't teach the boys?" It seemed a prying question, but by the way his shoulders tensed, the answer seemed obvious. She moved in front of him, wanting to see his face. "You have, haven't you? Whoa. I'm sorry. I shouldn't have asked."

"No, it's okay," Nash replied, although it was clear it wasn't.

"It doesn't look okay. Really, it's none of my business. I don't know when to keep my mouth shut sometimes."

"It's why I'm here." His words were quick and quiet, like ripping off a bandage. If a flinch had a sound, it was his tone. "Well, part of why I'm here. And, yes, it's why I won't teach the class."

"I'm so sorry. What happened?"

He turned to look at her, pain and memory and a bit of bewilderment in his eyes. There was something different about Nash's eyes, some subtle distinction she couldn't quite name but saw all the same. "The short version is that I used to work with teens. One of them, someone I had come to trust, turned on me. With a gun. I was shot once in the shoulder and once in the thigh. So you can see why I'm in no hurry to hang out with teenage boys right now."

"I didn't know. And here I've been egging you on like an idiot. I'm sorry."

"It could have been a lot worse. I try to thank God every day I'm still here. But the truth was, after that I couldn't stay in LA." He leaned against the porch railing as if the mere mention of the wound made his leg hurt. "I used to be able to see the good in some of the worst kids. I thought of it as my gift—cutting past all the trash talk and tough-guy tattoos to connect with guys before they went all the way bad."

"That does sound like a gift," Ellie said, meaning it.

"Yeah, well, two weeks in a hospital can knock the gift right out of a guy, I suppose."

For all her betrayed feelings, Ellie couldn't say Derek had actually *set out* to hurt her. To have someone seek to harm you, hunt you down at gunpoint? To fire at you with a mind to end your life? If she'd wanted to run from Atlanta, who wouldn't want to run all the way from California to get away from something like that?

Teens had hurt him. Of course he'd say no to working with them again. "I can see why you won't help Pastor Theo with those boys."

Nash shook his head. "'Why I won't help.' Why do those words bug me so much, making me feel petty for refusing to step up and lend a hand when I have every good reason to say no?"

Maybe Theo was right and God really was putting a plan together. "Are you sure you need to say no? Maybe you're just scared to say yes. Gran always says scared isn't a good enough reason to say no to something that might be good."

"Then your grandmother is a stronger person than I am."

What Nash did, helping those kids in LA, must have taken so much courage and compassion. It couldn't all be gone just because one kid betrayed him. Then again, wasn't she hiding here in Martins Gap because of betrayal, too? "What if what you really need is to prove to yourself you still can see the good in kids like that? What's the worst that could happen?"

He shook his head and gave a dark, low laugh. "I could get shot again. And this time the kid may not miss."

"Cowboys and Indians," she said, remembering his earlier comment that now had such a different edge to it.

"Cops and robbers," he said, his features showing a hint of humor.

"Cars and knitting." A plate of biscotti was on the porch table from her meeting with Pastor Theo. Ellie took one and held it in front of her like a mustache, doing a pathetic Groucho Marx impersonation. "It's an idea so crazy it just might work."

"It probably won't work." Nash took the cookie from her hands and took a big bite out of it. "But maybe I ought to try anyway."

Chapter Five

"Why, Ellie Buckton!"

Ellie smiled at the young woman behind the church office desk Thursday morning. With the exception of a few additional pounds and the switch from a perky ponytail to a more "adult" hairstyle, Dottie hadn't really changed. Frozen in time like half of Martins Gap, she presented a slightly older version of the high school friend she had been to Ellie. Of course, she was Dottie Howe now that she'd married Ted Howe, her high school sweetheart. Dottie was the mom of twins, but Ellie was embarrassed she couldn't remember their names or how old they were. She should have kept closer ties.

"Hi, Dottie."

"I heard you were back in town." Dottie shook her head and waved a hand adorned with bright pink fingernails. "Sorry to hear things didn't work out between you and the chef guy. So sad. I can't imagine what you're going through."

So word was out. That was to be expected—this

was prime, juicy gossip for the likes of Martins Gap. "Thanks." She still hadn't come up with a suitable reply for people's condolences. Ellie tried to tell herself that letting word spread through the rumor mill was better than having to rehash the painful details over and over, but her heart wasn't buying it. Dramatic as it sounded, these days she felt like emotional roadkill, forced to lie there in splatters while the rest of the world drove by and gawked. *This won't last forever*, she told herself. *Just for now. And everyone here is on your side. Remember that.*

"You remember the great big wedding Ted and I had. I can't imagine all that'd be involved in calling one off."

Ted and Dottie had married two weeks after high school graduation in a big affair by Martins Gap standards. Ellie had been a starry-eyed bridesmaid in the ceremony. Of course, after working in the Atlanta food industry, her idea of a big wedding was now a lot more elaborate than Ted and Dottie's VFW Hall reception. To Martins Gap, Derek's and her plans would have felt slick and sophisticated. Ellie put on her "I'm making the best of it" face and sighed. "Well, at least the invitations hadn't gone out yet." Those were sitting in a box back in her Atlanta apartment awaiting a stuffing-and-stamping-and-pizza-and-movie night that would have been next month with Katie, Derek, and Derek's brother and best man, Clark. Another casualty lying by the side of the road waiting to be cleaned up.

For a startled second she wondered if GoodEats had issued a press release. What an odd field public relations was in the restaurant world, where people were promoted as much as the food or the decor. "It's kind of a big mess right now."

"I am sorry. Must feel good to come back home for a spell."

Ellie could only shrug. "I'll let you know." Being on the ranch was one thing. Being out and about in Martins Gap felt like quite another. Everyone was friendly, but she couldn't help feeling on display knowing she was the object of whispers. Ellie changed the subject. "How are Ted and the kids?"

"Oh, they keep me running." She ran her hand over a framed photo of two sandy-haired, ruddy-cheeked boys who looked about four. "I work here while they're in preschool across the street. Why don't you come over for dinner one of these nights? Ted grills a mean steak and you can see the twins."

Your life is so different from mine, Ellie thought as she stared at the photo. The distance between the direction her life had taken and where Dottie's had led gaped wide between them. Dottie had called to say she was expecting, but Ellie had missed coming back for the baby shower. Ellie had knitted baby booties and sent them when the twins were born. She'd paid halfhearted attention to Dottie's social-media posts about fishing derbies and birthdays and lost teeth. There had been a few casual conversations when Ellie made it home, a wave at the grocery store last Christmas, but nothing substantial. "They're adorable," Ellie offered, because they were—all grins and freckles that matched Dottie's wide, welcoming smile.

"They make me crazy most days, but I wouldn't trade

them for anything." Dottie put down the file she had been holding. "It's a shame we've lost touch. I mean it about dinner, Ellie. You really should come." Her face brightened with an idea. "Two Fridays from now a bunch of us girls are getting pedicures and all kinds of stuff at Wylene's. We do it once every other month. We laugh ourselves silly. Lydia will be there, too. It's probably nothing like what you're used to, but it sure is fun. You ought to come."

Ellie's heart twisted at the invitation. With Dottie being so friendly, she knew she should be jumping at the offer, but it stung anyway. All but one of her high school friends were married—half of them mothers already. She'd be the only single woman in the crowd, the sad jilted city girl grafted in out of pity. "I'll think about it," Ellie replied.

"You do that. It's been ages since all of us have been together. It'd be a hoot. I know it would." She handed Ellie a scrap of paper. "Write down your cell-phone number and I'll get you all the details."

Ellie complied. "It's really nice of you to offer."

Dottie tore off another scrap of paper and scribbled down digits. "That's mine. I really do want us to get together. And you ought to come to Wylene's. You'd have fun, and I imagine you could use a little fun right now."

Ellie pocketed the number. "I suppose I could." *Say yes right now*, she told herself, but couldn't quite make the words come out. "I'll let you know. I'm here to see Pastor Theo."

"Oh, that's right. I plum forgot he said you were

coming in. You're going to do something for the after-school program he's got going."

Ellie smiled. "That's the plan."

"Good for you. You always did need to stay busy. I expect Martins Gap feels a bit slow and backward to someone with your kind of career."

"No, it's nice," Ellie replied. "I could use a break from things, you know?"

"Don't I know about needing a break! Well, anyways, Pastor's office is just in there. I'll bring you two coffee in a jiffy as soon as he's off the phone." She peered at a handset on the desk, tapping it as a red light blinked off. "And there he goes. Head right on in. He's expecting you. And I'm going to call you about dinner and Wylene's."

Ellie started walking toward the office. "Okay."

Dottie smiled one last time. "I bet Miss Adele's tickled to have you home for a spell. She talks about you all the time, you know. You and that big-city life of yours."

Me and that big-city life of mine. Now if only I knew what that life was going to be like from here. Anytime you want to let me in on Your plans, Lord, I'm listening.

Don looked up from a report he was filing. "Theo tells me you finally said yes to his request."

Nash had only called Theo this morning. The speed at which certain information traveled around this town still amazed him. "I did."

Don's chair gave a hearty squeak as he leaned back. "I know that can't have been easy for you, but I meant what I said to Theo. I think it'd be good for you and good for those kids. We all know you're a better choice than that fuddy-duddy old shop teacher they've got down at the high school."

Nash raised an eyebrow at the name-calling.

"One fuddy-duddy can call another fuddy-duddy out on his—" Don's eyebrows knitted together as he reached for the word "—fuddy-ness" He folded his hands over his portly stomach. "I know these kids don't relate to me. It's why I brought you in. I don't even understand half of what they're talking about anymore. My cell phone's only got numbers on it, and I like it that way. I'm just glad when I can work the radio in the cruiser and find the right website to file our reports."

In fact, Nash had been forced to step in three times last week to help Don navigate the state's online reporting system. Don was a good lawman—a very good one and highly respected by the adults—but the kids in town probably made fun of his outdated ways. That wasn't helpful. Kids who felt as though the sheriff's office was behind the times could easily jump to thinking they could outwit the local law. That led to stunts like what were happening at the Blue Thorn. Don had been smart to bring on a younger deputy, and Nash wanted to do a good job for the guy. It just felt as if it was going to cost him a whole lot to succeed.

"You told Theo about your background?"

For a guy who'd come to Texas to escape his past, he sure had been rehashing it a lot of late. "I did."

"Good. He'll support you. Good guy, Theo. Cares a lot about this town, and that goes a long way with me."

"Yeah," Nash agreed. "I like him. Killer recruiting

skills. Ellie told me no one ever says no to Pastor Theo. She looked at me like I had no choice once Theo had asked me."

"She's right. 'Course I knew that all along." Don snickered. "It might even have been why I suggested you."

Nash spun his chair to face Don. "*You* put Theo up to that?"

"It's in my best interest that you get acclimated into this community. You're no social butterfly, Larsen. I had to get creative."

Nash shook his head and turned back to his desk. At least if he was going to get railroaded into community service, it'd be alongside someone he liked and could relate to, like Ellie. If he'd ever wondered what made her hightail it out of Martins Gap, Nash had a feeling he was about to find out.

Chapter Six

Sheriff Mellows looked up at Ellie with a wide smile as she walked into the storefront that served as the Martins Gap Sheriff's Office. "Ellie, darlin', good to see you. You holding up okay?"

Everyone asked her that. Was she? Ellie didn't know. Nothing felt right, but parts of her still knew she'd made the right choice by breaking it off with Derek. "I think so" had become her standard reply to such questions. "I am glad to be home for a while, anyway." She switched subjects as quickly as possible. "Gran tells me this is your last term as sheriff. Are you really going to make Martins Gap elect someone new to fill those great big shoes?"

Mellows pointed to a small black gadget blinking the number 232 in red.

"Says right there. New sheriff takes over in two hundred and thirty two days, whoever he is. Or she. I'm a forward-thinking guy."

"You've got a countdown clock?" Ellie laughed.

"My granddaughter sent it to me from San Antonio. Nash says I've messed with it to make it run faster, but I'm amazed I got the fool thing to even turn on."

"Is Nash around? I just came from church and I have some stuff for the after-school program from Pastor Theo."

Don nodded toward the back door of the sheriff's office. "He's out back fiddling with that car like he does every lunch break. He may be putting poor old Clive out of a job tending to the department vehicles the way he keeps things running." He raised an eyebrow toward her tote bag. "I don't suppose you've got some of your Gran's brownies in that there bag?"

Gran kept the sheriff's office, the volunteer fire department and half a dozen other town services in baked goods. "Afraid not," she teased the older man. "But I have half a dozen blondie bars from Lolly's." Lolly's was the diner down the street known for its scrumptious deserts. "Will that do?"

Don laughed and patted the paunch straining his shirt buttons. "It will, darlin'. It'll do just fine. Don't you let Nash eat 'em all before I get some."

Ellie headed for the door that led out back. "I promise." The screen door gave a tired squeak as she pushed it open, causing Nash to look up from where he was bent over a low, sleek, black-and-gold sports car with the hood raised. The spring sun warmed the paved parking lot, and Nash was in a white cotton T-shirt, his uniform shirt hanging out of the way on a peg beside the door. A wide stripe of something black was smeared across one lean forearm while a matching smear ran across one side of his jaw. He offered her a cheerful grin as he worked a wrench around some nut or bolt on an engine part. "Hi, there. Give me a sec to get this tight and I'll be right with you."

She slid her bag onto the picnic table that sat in the shade cast by the office wall, noticing an open box from Shorty's Pizza on the table with a few slices gone. "Aren't you afraid you'll get engine grease on your lunch?"

He half grunted, half laughed as he struggled with the wrench. "I'm more afraid I'll get cheese on my spark plugs, actually. Ah, there." Whatever he was fighting with slipped into place, and he straightened up, reaching for a grimy towel spread across the front fender. "This is a nice surprise."

"I met with Theo this morning to go over the program schedule, and I thought I'd drop off a copy of the calendar he gave me." She'd tacked Lolly's and a visit to Nash on to the end of her errands as a present to herself for surviving the pitying stares of the bank teller—a woman who used to be in her high school chemistry class and who was now pregnant with her second child—and two whispering old ladies from the pharmacy. "I see you went to Shorty's. Has anyone introduced you to Lolly's blondies yet?"

Nash grabbed a cake of soap from above the hose spigot and turned on the water. "Not yet," he called above the noise of the water sloshing over his hands into a bucket on the pavement.

"Well, you're in for a treat. Half a dozen. Three for you, two for Don and one for me."

He dried his hands and came over and sat down on the picnic bench. "What if I only want one?"

Ellie pulled one of the large gooey squares out of the bag and broke off a corner. "You won't. Lolly's blondies are legendary. I've had Gran send them to me in Atlanta. Gran's tried to get her recipe for years, but Lolly's no fool." She bit into the sweet, crumbly delight. "Yum. If anyone ever tries to get out of a speeding ticket with one of these, take them up on it." Ellie threw a glance at Nash, who lowered his eyebrows at the suggestion. "Not that I was trying, that night. I just meant what I said—you really were the only nice thing in a really crummy day."

Ellie didn't like—or trust—the way her stomach flipped at the look Nash gave her in reply. She shifted her gaze to the car. "So that's the car, huh? Theo's right. It is a fancy thing."

Nash nodded and picked up another slice of pizza. "If you want to know where my money and my spare time go, you're looking at her."

"You must not have had much to move if you came out here in that. Does it even have a trunk?"

Laughing, Nash pointed at the rear of the vehicle. "It has a hatch. But, no, I wouldn't put that many miles on her. I had her shipped out. And as for belongings, yeah, I suppose you could say I travel light. My dad was navy, so we moved around a lot when I was growing up. I'm used to the shifting. LA was actually the longest I've stayed in one place."

Ellie ate another bite of the blondie. "Wow. I've lived two whole places in my entire life. Here and Atlanta.

I've never traveled abroad or anything—but I want to." She spread her hands. "I'd love to be a citizen of the world, you know?"

After a bite of pizza, Nash said, "It's not as great as it sounds."

"How can you say that?"

"My dad had a few posts in Asia. I was born in Japan, actually. My mom's Japanese."

Ellie looked at him, and suddenly the thing she couldn't name about his eyes became clear; they had just a bit of an almond shape to them. His coloring was ruddy, but his face had just enough of the round features and eyes to reflect a hint of Asian influence. Instead of clashing, the combination gave him a memorable, striking—okay, handsome—face.

Nash caught her looking and ran a hand through his golden-red hair. "You can imagine what it was like to grow up near Tokyo with this hair. I felt like a circus freak until fifth grade when we moved to Annapolis. I didn't have a peanut-butter-and-jelly sandwich until I was eleven years old. I'm probably the only person you know whose comfort food is sushi, not mac and cheese." He shook his head. "Martins Gap is sorely lacking in decent sushi joints, you know."

He picked up one of the blondies and bit into it. The confection lived up to its reputation, for pleasure washed over his face, and Ellie felt a surge of satisfaction for being the one to introduce him to one of the town's best goodies. "I think I found a way to cope," he said behind a mouthful. "These really are good."

* * *

Ellie was looking at him. "Martins Gap can be an adjustment, but it has its advantages. You'll find a way to fit in." She cocked her head, studying him. "You're not actually worried about that, are you?"

Nash couldn't come up with an answer that didn't make him appear either paranoid or insulting. "No, not really. Everyone's been welcoming. I like it here. And I chose to come here. It's just…"

"Not quite what you thought?" Ellie sighed. "I get that. It's not quite what I remember, either. And I haven't even been gone very long." She shrugged her shoulders. "Funny. I thought I'd feel foreign. I do. Then in other ways I don't. I feel like I don't fit in, but I feel *from* here. I can't really explain it." She shot him a look. "And I sure don't need to bore you with it."

"No," he said, surprised by how much he meant it. "I get it. You know you're different, but no one else seems to recognize it. Or they do, but not in the way you want."

Understanding lit the blue in her eyes. "Yeah, like that." She stood up, walked toward the car and peered under the hood. "It's a Japanese car, right? Is the manual in Japanese?"

Nash laughed. "No. And she takes good old American motor oil and gas."

She ran one hand down the line of the car's front panel, a soft stroke of artistic appreciation. "Does it go really fast?"

Nash pulled the rag from his back pocket and polished a smear off the front headlamp. "Officially, she never breaks the speed limit."

That pulled a smile from Ellie. "And unofficially?"

Nash couldn't suppress his own grin. "She's fast. And she corners like there's no tomorrow."

Ellie stepped over the toolbox to lean in the open window. "Is that an eight track? Like from the '70s?"

"It's a cassette player, actually. That was before our time, right? We're babies of the CD era, you and I."

"I'd be amazed if the kids in our program even know what a cassette tape is, much less an eight track. I mean, all they know are downloads and smartphones." She was babbling again. Maybe she was as unnerved by the easiness that seemed to spring up without warning between them as he was.

Some rebellious part of Nash liked that she'd said "our program." The way she'd said "you and I" a moment ago had uncurled something in his stomach that ought not be there. But she did look as though something was out of sorts—something beyond the broken engagement. "Did Theo say something? Are there concerns about the program? Or are you having second thoughts about taking such a long leave?"

"Second thoughts? Oh, about a million." She ran her hand along the chrome door handle, then down the rear fender, appreciating the car's bold lines. Nash always enjoyed it when people liked the Z as much as he did. It wasn't an antique, but it was an exquisite classic and a possession he treasured. "It was a dumb move, I suppose," she continued. "No one should hit the pause button on a great job like that. Only, I knew I couldn't stay. I couldn't stand everyone looking at me the way they did." She pulled her hand from the car to hug her chest. "There was no place there for me to hide and be hurt, you know?"

"I suppose."

She came back to the picnic table and sat down. "So why'd you bolt out of LA? I know you were shot and all, but why did you feel you had to move *so* far away?"

He made sure to keep a safe distance between them when he returned to the table, as well. "Well, for starters, I didn't bolt. The decision was a long, slow process. I had to think a long time before leaving."

"So you did like your job back there?"

"I did. I felt like I made a difference. It's not rocket science—gangs succeed because kids want to know they belong somewhere. They don't care that it's the wrong somewhere. Everyone throws their hands up like it's hopeless, but it's not. I've seen God do some amazing things in the worst kids' lives, Ellie. Tough guys everyone else would write off as good-for-nothings turned their lives around once they realized somebody actually cared about what happened to them."

"I could see where that would make a whole lot of difference."

"I'd get about one kid a year truly straightened out. And that would give me fuel to work on the other dozens who didn't. You have to be stubborn in my line of work."

Ellie put the last of her blondie in her mouth. "I guess so," she offered after she licked her fingers. "Derek used to say confidence was a chef's best trait—to believe he was captain of the kitchen and master of the ingredients and all." She rolled her eyes. "More like arrogance."

"He sounds like a real piece of work."

Ellie spread her hands as if introducing the guy on stage. "Derek Harding, Atlanta cuisine's rising star." She dropped her hands.

"Hector."

She looked at him. "Hector who?"

"Hector Forrio was the name of the kid who shot me." He hadn't even told Don that.

"Do you hate him? I hate Derek. I know I'm not *supposed* to hate him, and someday I'll probably just ignore him—I don't think the whole 'let's just be friends' thing is going to work here—but what I feel right now is pretty close to hate. I'm not proud of that, but I don't seem to be able to change it at the moment." She picked up the empty wax-paper wrapper that had held her blondie. "Hate tends to leave a bitter aftertaste. I'm self-medicating it with Lolly's blondies. I'm an 'eat my feelings' kind of gal."

He thought of the biscotti from the night of the traffic stop. "So I'm seeing." He took another bite of blondie in solidarity with Ellie. "I suppose I hated Hector for a while. When my shoulder hurts or I see the scars in the mirror, something still burns in my gut. But mostly I view him as more of a signpost. An arrow pointing out of LA, if that makes any sense. If it wasn't Hector, it would have been some other kid with some other name." That wasn't exactly true. Hector had been a special case. Nash's extraordinary connection with the boy—the trust he thought he'd built between them—was what let the hurt run so deep. And while he didn't drown his feelings in baked goods, he'd poured hundreds of dollars and hours into the car during his recovery. "I suppose you could say I'm a 'drive my feelings' kind of guy."

"Hey, you do what it takes to handle the Hectors and Dereks of this world. But you could have worked on your car in LA. I still don't get the move to someplace like here."

Nash sat back and leaned his elbows on the picnic table. "I needed somewhere far away and different. It could have been anywhere, really, but a friend knows Don's son and heard he was looking for a younger deputy to bridge the gap for consistency when the new sheriff was elected. The new sheriff can either keep me or bring in his own deputy, and I'm fine with that. The short time frame suits me fine." He managed a small laugh in spite of the serious conversation. "It's not like I did research."

"So you ended up here by accident?"

He didn't believe it was an accident, but he wasn't at a place where he could confidently say God had led him to Martins Gap, either. "Wouldn't Pastor Theo tell us to consider it providence?"

"Well, I know a good Christian woman would say I trust God's hand is at work in my failed engagement, but I'm afraid I'm not there yet."

Yes, it was smart to remember Ellie Buckton was a woman in the throes of serious rebound. A romantic land mine best kept in platonic territory. "It's been what, nine days? I think you're entitled to pitch a few fits."

She smirked. "Thanks. If you need anything hammered to bits, give me a call. I've got a lot of aggression to work out, and there are only so many holes you can dig on the ranch before the bison start to complain."

It was a good thing it was only a lunch break, or he might be tempted to remove the T-top inserts so that the Z was nearly a convertible and take Ellie out on the open highway. She'd like the way the wind and the engine noise could wash a problem off—for a little while, anyway. He'd come to depend on how a drive could blow off the residue a bad day could leave all over his mind and body. The unnerving notion that they weren't so different settled persistent and itchy in the back of his mind. Instead, he looked at his watch. "I'm back on shift in ten minutes. Thanks for the treats."

"Sure thing. I'll see you on the eighth, then?" The program was scheduled to start the first Wednesday after Easter.

He wasn't that surprised to realize he was looking forward to seeing her every week. This was going to take a little discipline on his part, especially if she kept plying him with baked goods and warm smiles. He rose and piled the rest of the blondies onto the pizza box while he picked up the files with his other hand. "Yep. See you then."

The little wave she gave as she headed out the office front door stuck with him for hours. That was not necessarily a good sign.

Chapter Seven

The crickets were singing loudly as Gunner's wife, Brooke, walked out on to the porch clutching a glass of ginger ale. "I don't need to read any test results to know this is a boy," she groaned as she eased herself into the wicker rocking chair. "No female would do this to another woman. It's got to be a boy. I was never this sick with Audie."

Ellie finished the last row of the sample squares she was knitting for the first girls' class next week. She'd found a clever pattern that took a small square and stitched it up into a slipper sock—an excellent first project for teen girls. It was a fun pattern to make up in bright colors of inexpensive yarn, but the resulting slipper socks would feel extra wonderful and last a long time if done in bison fiber. As such, they perfectly suited her program. "I'm sorry you've had such a rough time of it," she offered to her pale sister-in-law.

Brooke produced a weak smile. "I could say the

same for you. You were awfully quiet at dinner. Did something happen in town?"

Ellie put down the finished square and picked up her basket full of yarn. She moved over to the chair next to Brooke. "Shows that much, does it?" She reached into the basket and pulled out two balls of fluffy pastel yarn, one a sunny yellow and the other mint green. "I'll be okay. Which color do you like?"

Brooke considered a moment and then chose the green yarn. "I take it word's gotten out why you're home?"

Sitting back in her chair, Ellie fished the correct set of needles out of her case and began to cast on the required number of stitches for a baby-size version of the slipper sock. The sky was a still, perfect lavender dusk. The night had fallen soft and warm on such a jarring day. "It was bound to happen. I can't hide out at the ranch forever." She stopped stitching for a moment. "I just didn't count on feeling so...exposed. Like the whole world thinks they know my business, even though they only have half the story. It made me want to run around explaining the other half." She returned to the stitches. "Does that make any sense?"

Brooke sipped her ginger ale. "What's the half you think everyone knows?"

"Ellie Buckton's fiancé cheated on her with her best friend. Oldest story in the book, isn't it? It feels like everyone in Atlanta knew my relationship with Derek was on the rocks before I did. How can you feel that close to someone and in reality be so far away?" She'd cast on the full amount of stitches—not many for such a tiny pair of booties —and now turned the needles to start the first row. "I feel stupid. As if I was too dazzled to see Derek wasn't head-over-heels in love with me anymore—if he ever was at all. It's humiliating to think all my friends are all saying 'Poor, ignorant Ellie' behind my back."

"Don't you think there are some saying 'Ellie's better off without a cheating louse like Derek Harding'?" Brooke shifted uncomfortably in her chair. "I know that's what Gunner is saying. Quite a bit worse than that, if I'm honest."

Ellie managed a giggle. "Is it wrong that I love how ticked off Gunner is at Derek? Makes me feel…I don't know…defended." She continued stitching, delighting in the softness of the yarn and the hopeful feeling it gave her to make something for her coming nephew. She loved Audie, happily considered herself Audie's aunt, but to know the child to be born this September would be the first Buckton in so many years and the start of the next generation of Bucktons on the Blue Thorn? That was a blessing beyond counting. "I'm glad to think Gunner's in my corner, you know?"

"He's so happy to have you on the ranch. Your gran is and I am, too. But—" Brooke seemed to choose her next words carefully "—he knows you won't stay."

Ellie halted her stitching again. "I have to go back to Atlanta. I told him that the first night I was home. Who am I if I let a jerk like Derek drive me back home and away from my own life in Atlanta? I'm not saying I'll never come back, but today just showed me all over again why I left. I know you and Gunner are happy here, but this town is too small for me. I need bigger dreams than I can have here. I know Gunner understands that." Gunner certainly *should* understand that. He'd left the ranch for several years—run as far away from it as he could, actually—before coming back after their father died. Those had been tense, raw times. Ellie was glad things were completely different now.

"So you won't even consider staying? What about this venture with the bison fiber? Couldn't that be a big enough dream?"

Ellie waved the thought away. "It's a good side venture for the ranch and absolutely worth doing, but it's nothing I could build a career on. If it works—" she pointed one of the needles emphatically at Brooke "—and it *will* work—the most it can amount to is a steady project for me. A minor income stream, my bit for the family ranch, a hobby venture if you will."

"So why do it at all? It sounds like a lot of work for just a hobby."

"Because I've always wanted to. I've been toying with the idea since Gunner brought bison onto the ranch. It's a way to put my mark on the Blue Thorn the same way Gunner has put his. Okay, I admit part of the appeal is to prove Gunner wrong when he thinks it's silly."

"You're just going to make your point and then ride off into the sunset?" Brooke actually sounded disappointed.

Ellie finished the next row. "I'm going to make my point so I can have something that doesn't make me feel like a total failure." She turned her work and thrust the needle into the fabric to start a new row. "And then I'm going to go back and repair my trashed life in Atlanta. Find a real guy with solid values and no online fan base of foodie groupies."

That popped Brooke's eyes wide. "Foodie groupies? Really?"

"I ran the man's internet fan page, for crying out loud." Ellie leaned in. "I ran all the chefs' fan pages, actually. Which means I know how to take Derek's down in flames, if I wanted to… If I were a lesser woman, of course. I'm trying to take the high road here, but I won't say I haven't been tempted. He is, as you say, a cheating louse."

"You wouldn't publicly defame him." Brooke paused. "Would you?"

Ellie went back to stitching. "No. At least I don't think so." She pulled in a deep breath. "I mostly just want the whole thing to go away. I ran into my high school friend Dottie Howe today, with her happy family and her solid high-school-sweetheart marriage and her lovely but ordinary life, and I felt like some sort of failed social experiment. Local girl goes to big city and gets burned. She was so nice, but I couldn't help thinking she was looking at me like I'm some sort of social charity case. She invited me to dinner with the family and to girls' night out for pedicures at Wylene's."

Brooke stuck her swollen feet out in front of her. "Someone rubbing my feet while they soak in warm water? Sounds so wonderful. I'll go if you don't. I may need a pair of those slippers before the month is out just because I won't fit into any of my shoes anymore."

Brooke sighed and wiggled her pudgy toes before setting them back down on the porch boards. She gave Ellie a pointed look. "Do you know, yet, how it all fell apart with you and Derek? Do you have a sense of what went wrong?"

Ellie tucked her legs up underneath her and kept stitching. "I still love him, I think, but I also think I was in love with the idea of him more than the man he was. Part of me was drawn by Derek's huge personality—the talent, the notoriety, the intensity, all that stuff." Ellie turned a row, and the memory of Derek flooding her desk with roses the day after he proposed rose bright and vivid in her mind. He was enthralling, she'd give Derek that much.

"And that part of me blinded me to the bad side of his over-the-top nature—the tantrums, the need for attention, the blowups at even the smallest criticism, all those ego things chefs are known for. For a long time the roller coaster was fun—exhilarating, actually—but then when I had work pressures or wedding details that needed attention, he'd act like my problems or needs were too much for him to handle. As if it were my role to support Derek but not his role to support me."

"Did you fight a lot?" Brooke asked, picking up the green ball of yarn again and stroking it with such an air of maternal love that Ellie could only smile.

"I didn't think we argued more than any other couple, but looking back I suppose you could say yes. I expected Derek to pull his weight in the relationship, and I don't think he saw marriage that way. Work made it worse, too. My job at GoodEats was to support him, bolster his image, tout him to the press and all. His job was to be spectacular and promotable—and believe me, he was." She let the knitting drop to her lap. "It's just that he seemed to think those roles should carry over into our personal relationship. He'd get mad when I'd call him on dropping the ball on something. He wanted a fan, not a wife."

The deep truth of that realization caught her up short, raising a lump of pain and regret in her throat. "I guess he found one in Katie. She is a sous chef at another of our restaurants, and I always felt she was a little starstruck by Derek, but I didn't…" Suddenly she didn't want to finish that sentence. She wiped one eye with the back of her hand and sniffed as she picked up the knitting again. "Well, you know."

"I'm sorry they hurt you like that."

Keep stitching. Keep creating. Keep moving forward away from the pain. "You and me both, sister."

"I hope next week with the volunteer program goes really well for you," Brooke offered, still touching the soft ball of yarn. "I think it's your turn to have a few fans."

As she kept stitching and watched the stars come out over the herd and the pastures, Ellie said a prayer that next week's class would be fun and uplifting, not another reason to lick new wounds.

Nash had never been especially good with audiences, and today was proving no exception. The semicircle of eight boys gathered near the garage at the back of the church parking lot. Their "you'd better make this interesting" stares made Nash gulp. He'd clearly made a mistake in assuming the boys in his program would *want* to be here. These eight—sprawled across their chairs and glancing between him and their cell phones—looked as if they were in detention, even though Pastor Theo had told him this was voluntary. If this was voluntary, Nash dreaded to see what mandatory looked like.

He cleared his throat, earning a shred of attention from half of the group. "A few ground rules before we get started." That earned groans of disapproval. "First, no phones." The groans became yelps of protest. "Second, everybody gets their hands dirty." That earned a few "well, duhs!" from the guys. "Third, everyone gets a chance to drive."

Jose, a husky kid with thick black hair and angry eyes, looked up from his phone. "I got no car, so what am I gonna drive?"

Nash had been waiting for that question. He grabbed the handle of the garage door behind him and said, "This." With that, he pulled the door up to reveal his shiny Z that he'd backed into the church garage earlier this afternoon.

"Whoa," said Billy, who had clearly been proud of the old pickup he'd parked in the church lot ten minutes ago. "You kidding?"

"No, I'm not. But each of you is going to have to earn the chance to get behind this wheel." Nash walked toward the car, pleased to see all the boys get up and follow him. The Z was a stunner of a car, and he planned to use that to its full advantage. "One hundred thirty-two horsepower may not sound like much today, but she was built to be fast and still is. Her aerodynamics were groundbreaking for the time. Only twenty-five hundred of these were ever made, so she's a limited edition, gentlemen." He figured the lure of a chance to drive this would earn him loads of cooperation, and based on the looks on the boys' faces, that would be true.

"That's your car?" Leon, a beanpole of a guy with freckles, asked with wide eyes.

"It is."

"And you're just gonna let us drive it?"

Nash opened the driver's side door. "No, I'm gonna let each of you *earn* the chance to drive it. And I expect each of you can and will."

"Why would you let us drive your fancy car? We could wreck it," asked Mick, the toughest-looking boy of the bunch. The kid looked suspicious, as if no one had ever trusted him with anything valuable. It was a face Nash recognized from boys in LA—a symptom of how low expectations of young men usually were bound to come true. Step one was always to set a high expectation, communicating the idea that these kids had potential. It always twisted his heart what a foreign concept that was for many young men—no matter what city or state.

With that, Nash opened the car door wider and gestured for Mick to sit in the driver's seat. Mick gave a classic "who, me?" balk, but then jumped right in to take his place behind the wheel. "You like cars. Guys who like cars can respect them. If you all show me you can respect the car we're going to rebuild, then I'll know you can respect a car like this. Once I know you'll treat her right, I'm happy to share the Z with you. But," he continued, giving them his best "tough cop" glare, "if you show me, our project car or this car any disrespect, then I won't let you behind this wheel. Do we have a deal?"

Heads nodded around the room. Establishing a joint partnership was always step two. A goal—one that was separate and more tangible than "stay out of trouble"— got everyone on the same team. The Z was a big, snazzy and powerful incentive—provided it didn't get stolen or rolled by the end of the program. Based on the looks filling the boys' faces, Nash was pretty sure his baby was safe.

"Want to hear how she sounds?" When heads nodded again, Nash motioned for Mick to come out of the car, then slipped into the driver's seat and gunned the ignition. The lush, throaty roar of the car's engine filled the garage, gaining looks of admiration and outright envy from the boys, as Nash had known it would. The Z wasn't flashy in a rich-guy "look at me" way, but she was gorgeous in a classic way any car guy could appreciate. And these were car guys in the making.

But, like most boys their age, they thought they knew everything. And that was the first thing that had to change. Nash killed the engine and popped the hood latch. He gathered the boys around the front of the car as he propped the long hood on its support rod and began pointing to various engine parts. "Who can tell me what that is?"

"The radiator."

"And that?"

"That's where the spark plugs are."

On it went for twenty minutes, a game of informational one-upmanship between the boys that gave Nash a perfect glimpse of how much the guys already knew. It also told him a lot about the dynamics of the group, such as who took charge, who started arguments, who backed down when challenged and who bluffed when he didn't know. It shouldn't have surprised him how some things about teenage boys were universal. What did surprise him, as he drew out details of their home and school life, was how little attention it seemed these boys received from their parents; he'd expected the rural happy-family model to rule the day out in the country like this. The load of family problems, broken homes, economic hardships the boys hinted at even on this first day stunned Nash. *Serves me right for making assumptions*, he chided himself as he handed out a worksheet at the end of the day.

"Homework?" Davey, the quietest of the bunch, and the one who actually seemed to know the most about engines, finally piped up in obvious protest. "You gotta be kidding me."

"Relax. It's not homework," Nash replied.

Jose squinted at the paper. Did the boy need glasses and not have them? "Looks like homework to me."

"I want each of you to tell me about your dream car. If I were to hand you a million dollars tomorrow, what car would you buy? Go research that car. Tell me the options you'd get, fill in the specs for fuel consumption, brake horsepower, torque, all the goodies. Even the color—interior and exterior. As many details as you can find. That's not homework, now, is it, boys?"

Billy looked up from the worksheet. "What would you buy, Deputy Larson?"

"You can call me Nash. What car would I buy? You're looking at her."

"You have a million dollars?" Doug gawked.

"No, I don't need a million dollars. I want a car I can work on and drive anywhere, and for me, that's this car, not a fancy Lamborghini or some other European number. That's the thing about cars. I said you *could* spend a million for your dream car, but you don't *have* to. Would I drive a Lambo? In a minute. It'd be fun to drive. But would I want to own one? Not so much. See you next week, dream car papers in hand."

"Sixty-five Mustang," Davey offered as he stuffed the worksheet in his pocket, making Nash suspect it would show up next week with grease stains and tattered edges. "Red."

As they headed out of the garage, the boys started in on a boisterous argument over what the ultimate dream car was. They'd only grunted at each other when they had come in. Already they were getting better at communicating as a group. It had begun. He'd gotten a toehold on the project. From here anything was possible. Nash recognized the spark of satisfaction deep in his chest—a sensation he'd been pretty sure was gone from his life. *Thank You, Lord*, he prayed as he folded up the chairs against the garage wall. *You know how much I needed that*.

He'd just closed the hood on the Z when Ellie walked

into the garage looking a bit frazzled. "How'd it go?" she asked in a high, tight voice.

Nash would have said "great," but her expression made him take it down a notch to "Pretty good, actually. How about you?"

Ellie chewed her bottom lip. "In all honesty, I'm not so sure." She took a few steps toward him. "They *want* to be here, don't they? I mean, this wasn't forced on them, right?"

Nash wiped his hands as he walked over to her. "You haven't worked with teens before, have you?" Knowing her, she'd expected everyone instantly to share her enthusiasm for crafts, to be as eager to learn as she was. Teens could get there, but they usually hit you with a lot of apathy before they engaged. And really, hadn't he had the same thought about the boys' reluctant attitudes? "They test you at first, hide any enthusiasm, even if they really are interested."

"Oh, these girls were hiding their enthusiasm, that's for sure. One girl—Marny?—she had what Gran calls 'the eye of death' down pat. I've never felt so much bored annoyance in the space of ninety minutes."

She looked crestfallen. She'd probably done a great job with those girls, even if she didn't realize it yet. Ellie was authentic, and kids recognized that and connected with it—they just rarely showed it. He searched for something he could say or do to cheer her up or at least distract her. "I'm hungry," he offered, looking at his watch. "Want to show me where the best barbecue is in town?"

"Buck's is good, but it's Wednesday night. Everyone will be there." Her words declared loud and clear that she didn't care for *everyone's* company right now.

"So, who's got the best barbecue *out* of town?"

Her eyes caught on to what he was suggesting. "Red Boots. About twenty miles east of here. But you don't want to drive all that way."

"You clearly don't know about car guys. A nice drive on a warm spring night on a back country road? You don't have to ask me twice. Come on."

Chapter Eight

Ellie lifted her hands over her head through the car's open T-top roof, letting the warm summer air flood around her fingers. *Freedom.* It felt like freedom to be barreling down the road, away from the bored-looking girls, away from everything that wasn't working in her life, away from all the prying eyes in Atlanta and Martins Gap. *Away.* She'd fled back to Martins Gap thinking she was escaping, only to discover her problems and shortcomings followed wherever she went.

Nash glanced over at her and smiled. He was having fun, too, pointing out how the car handled certain curves, opening up the engine on straightaways and generally being a kid showing off his favorite toy. She was almost sorry when he pulled the sports car into a parking place at the crowded Red Boots Grill—the temptation to tell Nash to just keep driving off into the sunset pulled hard on her tired spirit.

"You enjoyed that," Nash said as he walked around

and opened the car door for her. Ellie had forgotten guys even did that anymore—Derek never had. For all Derek's modern pizazz, there was something to be said for good old-fashioned manners. "I'm glad."

"It was fun. I feel like the wind washed all the knots out of my neck." She tried to tamp down her windblown hair, then gave up. *There isn't anybody in the Red Boots who would know me anyway, so who cares what my hair looks like right now?*

"That's what I feel when I drive her—washed off. Some days I think I can almost see the stress lying scattered on the road in my rearview mirror." He flushed, running a hand through his own tousled hair. "That sounds cheesy, doesn't it?"

They both must look like windblown scarecrows. It was wonderful not to care. "Not a bit." She nodded up at the sign—a neon-red boot that kicked. "Hope you're hungry."

"Starved. Disgruntled teens always make me hungry."

Ellie laughed. "Disgruntled. That's a good name for what those faces looked like. A cross between grumpy, bored and unimpressed. I've faced hostile catering clients that were an easier sell."

Nash opened the door for her. "Do you care about the girls? About what they think and whether or not they're getting anything out of your time together?"

"Of course I do. Why would I do this if I didn't think they would enjoy knitting and get the same things out of it that I do?"

"Then that's what matters. They're just testing you

to see if you *really* care. And you do. They'll figure that out and come around. Trust me."

"Name?" a scrawny girl in a red shirt asked from the hostess desk.

"Natsuhito," Nash replied in a totally ordinary voice.

Ellie and the girl both blinked at the strange name.

"Wanna spell that?" the hostess asked, clearly stumped. "Or should I just say Nat?"

Nash leaned over the clipboard. "*N-A-T-S-U-hito*. Just like it sounds." Ellie watched in astonishment while Nash smirked like a kid in on a joke.

When they'd moved aside to the waiting area, Ellie raised an eyebrow at him. "Natsu-what-o?"

He leaned back against the wall and crossed one foot over the other. "Natsuhito. You didn't think Nash stood for Nashville, did you?"

"*That's* your full name?"

"The Japanese part. My full name is Natsuhito Joshua Larson. Natsuhito was my mother's grandfather's name, and Joshua came from my dad's side of the family." He nodded back toward the hostess. "I pull it out for fun now and then."

As if on cue, the hostess looked right at them and drolled out "Nash-tu-hillo party?"

Ellie found herself laughing as the hostess led them to a booth. "I thought we were being incognito tonight," she remarked as she slid into the red leather seats.

Nash slid in across from her, the smile still lingering on his features. "We are. Nobody will ever know Natsuhito is us. And we needed to have some fun."

"You're one surprise after another, Nash-tu-hito."

"Nat-su-hito," he corrected. "And *Nash* will be just fine. I think most people in Martins Gap would choke at the name if I used it there anyway."

"Maybe not," Ellie countered. "Sure, it's a small town in the middle of Texas, but they're a welcoming lot. They won't care much where you came from."

The server set down big plastic glasses of water and Nash took a long drink. "So now you're defending the place? Before it sounded as if you couldn't get out of there fast enough."

"Oh, Martins Gap can be annoying and quirky sometimes, but it's still home. I just needed more… possibilities than I could see here. The ranch was always Gunner's thing—even when he ran away from it for a bunch of years. I want to do something to support the family business, but I need to make my own mark in the wider world. One that's much wider than here." She exhaled and fiddled with the place mat. "I'm not even sure my future will be at GoodEats Inc. anymore, either."

"Because of what happened with Derek?"

"Here's some biscuits," said the server as she set down a big plate of fluffy, crusty squares. "Y'all ready to order?"

Nash looked at Ellie for guidance. "I've got this," she said to him before turning to the server. "A pound of fatty brisket, a pound of ribs, coleslaw and corn. And two root beers." She raised an eyebrow at Nash. "They make the best root beer in the state just up the road and serve it here—do you like it?"

Nash shrugged his shoulders. "It's been a dozen

years since I've had the stuff. I can't remember." He looked up at the server. "Why not?"

The server left, and Ellie pulled her silverware from its red napkin wrapping. "You're about to find out what real Texas barbecue is supposed to taste like. It's going to ruin the rest of the country for you, just know that." She slathered butter on one of the biscuits and took a bite. "Oh. Yep, nothing will ever come close after Red Boots. And I'm in the food biz, so I claim a hunk of expertise here."

"That's mighty big hype for a hunk of beef. Someone might think you were in marketing."

Ellie laughed before taking another bite of biscuit. The tension of the afternoon began to slough off her neck and shoulders—whatever tension was left after that marvel of a car ride. Her brother Luke always talked about his motorcycles in terms of how the ride made him feel, and now she could begin to understand what he meant. Good food and pleasant company just added to the whole relaxing effect. She didn't know Nash that well, but found him delightfully easy to talk to despite their stressful introduction.

"You were telling me what happened with Derek and your job."

His cue yanked her back down to earth. "It's probably the oldest story there is—guy cheats on girl with girl's best friend. And the work thing just made it worse. I like working at GoodEats, I do. It's just that, well, I never really felt like one of the team. I know I'm just starting out, but all the other staff seem to be these sophisticated, big-city types. Some days I feel like an invader from cowboy-land masquerading as a marketing professional."

Nash took a biscuit. "You must be good at your job if they're willing to hold it for you while you're here."

"I hate to admit it, but I think that might have been Derek's doing. He pulls a lot of weight around there." Ellie sat back. "I was so amazed when he first began to take notice of me. Little Ellie from nowhere catching the eye of the star chef. Here was a guy who'd been all over the world, who wore Italian suits and got hundred-dollar haircuts, but still went to church and loved grilled-cheese sandwiches. I thought he was amazing, and for him to notice me made me feel special, you know? Like I'd arrived in the real world to have this big-time chef—who could have anyone—want to be with me. I fell hard. He knew how to woo a girl, that's for sure. It was like something out of a movie. Gifts, fancy events, romantic dinners on his rooftop deck and flowers—boy howdy, did that man know how to send flowers. When Derek proposed, I was over the moon."

A mountain of meat, piled high on white butcher paper alongside tubs of coleslaw and creamed corn, appeared at the table. Nash took in the scope of the enormous meal and grinned. "You weren't kidding about the hungry part."

"Well," she replied, not even needing a knife to separate a chunk of the oh-so-tender brisket to pull toward her side of the paper landscape laid out between them, "leftovers are pretty much a given when you come here. Gunner insists it's the best breakfast ever, but that may be a guy thing." She put the tangy, splendid meat in her mouth. "Forget everything you know about nutrition and just enjoy."

Nash pulled off a hunk for himself, and Ellie had fun watching his reaction to the barbecue. "Wow," he said, his eyes closing in carnivorous delight. "This definitely lives up to the hype." He looked at her. "You're right. Everything else that claims to be barbecue after this is just going to seem like a knockoff to me."

Ellie chuckled. "It's always a hoot to watch someone get their first taste of Red Boots. I suppose it's kind of a rite of passage around here. I'm surprised no one's taken you before this. You've been in town what—a little over two months?"

Nash leaned on one elbow. "I haven't exactly been social. I suppose I've been keeping to myself while I figure things out."

"Things like what?"

"I was all about the job and the cause in LA. I was totally committed to my work and the kids. Lots of the guys I worked with had my home phone number and my cell, and they would call me at all hours when they got in trouble." She watched his face change, a fierceness tightening his features with the memories. "It wasn't an imposition—I liked it. I liked how they felt they could count on me, especially since these were guys who weren't used to being able to rely on anyone. I could relate to that. We moved so much growing up I didn't really have buddies, no guys I knew had my back. I felt a real calling to be that for some of those boys. They knew I was all in for them, and it's what enabled some of them to break free of the gang hold and try for a better life. I felt like my commitment showed them they could belong somewhere else than in a gang."

"You must have made such a difference in their lives." Listening to him talk, all her efforts at GoodEats seemed trivial. He had changed lives, and all she'd ever changed was this month's pasta-special campaign. "That must feel good."

"It did." He reached for one of the ribs. "But you know what they say—the people you let closest are the ones who can hurt you the most."

Ellie dug into the tub of coleslaw. "Derek made sure I learned that lesson."

"Where did things go wrong between the two of you? Or don't you want to talk about it?"

How many nights had she sat up pondering that question? She was fine if she kept busy during the day—which wasn't hard to do on the ranch—but nights were another thing. Lying in bed, she had trouble shutting down her brain's constant dissection of her and Derek's relationship. The answers she came up with only made her feel worse. "No," she replied. "It's okay. I spend so much time thinking about it that talking it out might help. With someone who's not family, I mean. Gunner, Brooke and Gran love me, I know, but their advice isn't what I need right now, you know?"

"I get that. For what it's worth, I've got no advice whatsoever for you." He licked sauce off his sticky fingers. "So feel free to bore me with all the juicy details."

Nash watched Ellie pull off more brisket with a deliberate, artistic hand. He just piled meat on his side of the paper, but Ellie arranged it. "The way I see it," she began, "it boils down to the truth that Derek and I each liked the idea of being married to each other, but in reality, we wanted something different."

Nash wasn't quite sure what that meant. "You're gonna have to explain that."

She gestured wildly as she talked. "I wanted a fancy guy. Sophisticated, a man of the world. Successful, well dressed, the whole package. And Derek was that. It's just that the mind-set that came with it? That never sat right with me, even when I tried to convince myself that's how successful people think and behave. Derek saw no reason to meet my family before he proposed— and didn't expect me to meet his family, either. Except for Gunner's wedding, he could never find time to come out here—not that I wasn't guilty of the same thing. I missed a lot of chances to come back to the Blue Thorn because I was too busy making us into Atlanta's next power couple. Ha-ha on me." She gave a dark, bitter laugh as she dunked a hunk of brisket into the pool of sauce.

"And then?"

"It started showing up in the wedding plans. He wanted big and splashy, the best of everything—which makes sense. I mean, Derek's taste and flair are what make him who he is."

Her confidence really had taken a hit from this guy. "Hey, you have taste and flair."

"Have you ever read the real estate ads?"

Nash couldn't quite see what that had to do with the current topic of conversation. "No."

"The small, sensible houses—the ones that are good enough but not showstoppers—have you ever noticed they are always called 'charming'?" Her eyes narrowed at the last word.

"No."

"Well, they are. And to Derek, everything I did and everything I liked was charming. He wanted to push me over into spectacular—that was his turf. He was always shifting my preferences a bit here, tweaking my choices a bit there, redoing everything. I thought it was attentiveness. I didn't recognize it was for the revision it was. He was making me over into someone who could be his partner, and I let him. I liked it. He changed my hair, where I shopped for clothes, even how I drank my coffee. He called my knitting 'charming' and 'Ellie's quaint little hobby.'" The edge in her eyes showed how unforgivable she found that last remark, and Nash made a mental note never to use the words *charming* or *quaint* in her presence—certainly not to describe anything she loved as much as knitting.

"Katie? Now, she was all elegance and style," Ellie continued. "Everything that was effort for me came naturally to her. I felt fancy and important having her for my best friend. I thought we balanced each other out, the same way Derek and I balanced each other out."

Nash could see where this was headed. No wonder Ellie seemed to have lost her nerve—this Derek idiot clearly had decided he was better served by "trading up." Nash had met women like Katie—even dated some of them until the shellac of their personalities had worn thin. He didn't have to meet this Katie to know he wouldn't like her and wouldn't ever find her as authentic and genuine as the woman in front of him licking barbecue sauce off her fingers. He started to say something, but then decided it was better just to let Ellie keep talking.

"At first he told me what he liked best about me was how different I was from him. I guess it became just too much effort to bridge the gap between us." Her eyes glistened with the threat of tears. "On the really bad days I wonder if he just was ashamed of me, if I was some country girl he'd taken on as a project, whose amusement factor wore off when I couldn't be fancied up enough."

Was it any wonder Nash had found her barreling down the highway back home that night? Her eyes were filled with hurt that ran way deep. He had a thing or two to say about Derek's supposed taste.

"We really thought we loved each other. I bought into the whole Prince Charming fantasy, you know?" Ellie swiped at her eye with a corner of her napkin. "Sorry. I'm still broken up about it."

Clearly. She was a mess—and deserved to be. "Hey, it's okay."

"And it's bad enough about Derek, but Katie? Her, too? What kind of best friend does that? How is it ever okay to betray someone like that?"

Nash had been fascinated with women before, but never in love enough to propose marriage. He didn't know how it felt to be engaged—or to have it all fall apart. The sting of betrayal, however? That he could relate to easily. How it dug right down to the bones, how it made you second-guess everything you thought you knew about people and relationships. "It's never okay to betray someone like that, Ellie. If either one of them could do that to you, they don't belong in your life or your heart." He hadn't meant to make a declaration like that, but the look in her eyes pulled it out of him.

"Suddenly all my friends' comments about 'I never expected the two of you to get together' and 'I guess opposites really do attract' made a bit too *much* sense. When word got out—and you can imagine how quickly it did—everyone was very sympathetic and sad, but they all had that little edge of...un-surprise that just made me want to die. As if no one had ever really expected it to work out in the first place." She pulled in a deep breath. "Honestly, I felt like everyone had these comforting words, but behind them they were all just thinking 'Nice try' and 'I could have told you so.'"

He knew what it was like to feel as if someone had painted *failure* on his back. Sure, he had known many successes in his work with the teens in LA, but the one teen who had turned and shot him seemed to wipe all the rest off the map. Was it so hard to see how this one "failure" knocked Ellie's confidence in all aspects of her life?

She ran her finger down the side of her glass of root beer, making a little swirly trail in the condensation— even her fidgets were artistic. "I feel like I can't do anything right. I mean, I know that's not true, but I don't trust my judgment. If I can be so wrong about something as big as planning to spend the rest of my life with someone like Derek, and everyone else could see what I couldn't, then what can I count on? How can I trust myself or my choices?"

"So it's not really all about the bison fur, is it?" Even he could see this endeavor was just Ellie's way of finding her confidence again. That didn't make it wrong or silly; it just explained her over-the-top passion for something that didn't strike him as especially urgent.

"Not fur—the fiber's called bison *down*, actually. And, yes, I suppose it's about a lot more than just Blue Thorn Fibers."

"Oh, so you've picked out a name already."

She blushed. The pink in her cheeks did the most amazing thing to the color of her eyes. Nash chose to ignore the gentle thudding that had started in his gut. That, and the growing certainty that this Derek was a first-class fool who liked a slick, superficial life instead of real worth and didn't know a good, honest treasure when he had one.

"I certainly couldn't let Gunner do it. He's terrible at naming things. I can see the whole thing clearly in my head, you know. The colors, the weights, a few silk blends for the really fancy stuff, everything. People will pay a lot of money for good bison fiber."

Nash couldn't help himself. "Okay, so I have to ask. What kind of good money?"

"I've paid over seventy dollars for a really good skein of one hundred percent bison. It's soft and light and strong—"

"Seventy dollars? For *yarn*?"

That got her back up. "And worth every penny. Can

you sit there and tell me you haven't paid good money for quality car parts?"

There was an ashtray fixture he'd just ordered from Japan sitting in his garage ready to call that bluff. "Well, I suppose I see your point." It was good to see the fight rise in her eyes—defeat didn't become Ellie Buckton at all. "But I don't see how the girls fit in to making the case for Blue Thorn Fibers. You wouldn't really give such expensive stuff to girls just learning, would you?"

"On the drive out here, you said you told the boys they could drive your car if they earned the right. This is the same thing. But more than that, I want them to help us make it. Maybe you saw the brushes we set up in the pastures when you were out there with Gunner. We used those to…" She put her hand up. "You're not really interested in all the technical mumbo jumbo. I know I tend to—and this was Derek's favorite term for it—overshare."

Again, this Derek jerk had taken what was one of her best qualities—her enthusiasm—and labeled it a fault. *You're so much better off without him*, his brain yelled at the woman gleefully selecting her next rib, but he kept silent.

"I always teach with good quality fiber and needles. It makes the whole experience so much more satisfying. Learning goes faster, and the results are always better. Surely you can see that."

Based on what he'd learned about his boys, he could see the flaw in her thinking. He had to tread carefully with what he said next. "I'm not so sure these girls have the cash to work with seventy-dollar yarn."

Ellie sat back. "Of course they don't. Which is why they'll help us make it. They'll earn their yarn by the end of the program. What they're working with now I paid for out of my own pocket." When Nash took a breath, she held up a hand again. "Don't start. I know that's not how it's supposed to work, but Theo didn't give me nearly enough money to do this right, and you said so yourself, this is about more than just yarn. I need this to work. I don't mind the expense just this once."

Nash looked at Ellie and the energy practically zinging out of her fingertips. This woman never did anything halfway or "just this once." How was she ever going to slide through these weeks and just hop on back to Atlanta?

That's not your problem, he told himself during dinner and on the drive home through the stunning night sky. *Don't make it your problem, either.*

Chapter Nine

A bell clanged loudly Friday night as Ellie pushed open the door to Wylene's Beauty Spot. The place hadn't changed one molecule since Ellie's high school days. Wylene stood in one corner arranging hair-care products. She wore a pale pink smock embroidered with her name on one side in swirly letters. Her head was piled high with a mountain of yellow-white hair so shellacked in place that as a child Ellie had believed Wylene took it off at night like a motorcycle helmet. The shop owner gave up a hoot and waved her arms. "Ellen May Buckton, as I live and breathe." She shifted back on one hip and took in Ellie from head to toe. "Well, look at you, all citified."

Each of the six women in various stages of various treatments looked up with various degrees of welcome. Ellie, in a pair of cropped khaki pants and a patterned shirt that wouldn't draw any attention in Atlanta, looked at the collection of young moms in T-shirts, jeans, yoga pants and ponytails. She had known each of these women when they were all teenagers, yet the older, parental faces they had now made them seem like total strangers. She'd talked herself into coming here— determined to make more substantive connections with Martins Gap's twentysomethings—but now doubted the choice. She was the same age as these women, but Ellie didn't feel nearly old enough to be a mom, much less a mom to twins like Dottie was. It had been a mistake to come. "Hi, y'all," Ellie said as she waved, hoping her reluctance didn't show in her meek greeting.

"Dottie has filled us in about your unfortunate heartbreak," Wylene commiserated. With a gulp Ellie remembered Wylene was on husband number four. "There's no better balm for a broken heart than pretty toes and fingernails. Unless you want to go dramatic and become a redhead or some such thing."

"LuAnn Marker did just that," said a woman from the pedicure chair in the corner. Ellie eventually recognized her as cheer captain Lydia Jacobs. "She cut her hair short and dyed it bright red when Archie joined the army." Lydia, once the owner of long blond tresses half the high school boys had drooled over, now sported a sensible bob. "'Course, LuAnn always was one for the drama, bless her heart."

"One of my finest hours," Wylene boasted as she led Ellie toward a chair. "It was like watching a phoenix rise from the ashes, it was." Without asking, she began running her fingers through Ellie's hair. "That man was thunderstruck when he came home for Christmas. They named the baby after me that fall."

Laughter filled the room. "They did not!" called

Dottie from the manicure table. "That baby's name is Walter."

"Well, you can't very well name a boy Wylene, now, can you?" Wylene returned to her examination of Ellie's hair. "I got the W, and that's all I need." She clicked her tongue. "Darlin', what have you been doing to this hair? It's as dry as a hay bale."

Ellie had seen enough salon breakup disasters to know now was not the time to ponder a dramatic change in her hair. "I'm always busy at work," she offered. She'd been growing her hair out so she could put it up for the wedding, so it probably did look a bit shaggy. She and Katie had planned a spa day for next month to start getting Ellie ready for the wedding. One more thing to cancel. "I really just want to do my nails tonight. Nothing else."

"You sure? Give me two hours and I can make you positively dreamy." Wylene tilted Ellie's chin this way and that as if collecting ideas. "Those Buckton eyes. What a color. My sister in Galveston says you can buy contacts to turn your eyes that blue even if they're brown. Can you imagine?"

Ellie had disliked her turquoise eyes and honey-colored hair as a child. They marked her identity before she ever said one word. Back then she hadn't liked being just "another Buckton," but now she held great affection for the family characteristic. She loved her family—most of the time. She just often felt overshadowed or misunderstood by them. It hadn't been that much fun to be sandwiched between a memorable brother like Gunner and dynamic twins like Luke and Tess.

"Long layers?" Wylene persisted. "Maybe highlights to really make those eyes sparkle?"

"No, thanks, Wylene. Not today. Maybe in a few weeks." She'd committed now to the six weeks of the girls' knitting classes, but after that, where would she be? Even if she chose to end her career at GoodEats, Atlanta apartments weren't that hard to sublet—she could end up just about anywhere.

Dottie came up to them, holding her hands upright to protect the fresh manicure. "Now, Wylene, our Ellie's smart enough to avoid the trap of breakup hair. Don't you go nudging her toward anything drastic." She wiggled her bright pink fingernails. "Keep the red to your fingers and you'll do fine. Here, take my station while I dry."

Ellie sat in the manicure chair and spread her fingers on the small counter. Her eyes fell upon the empty spot on her left hand and the familiar sting returned to her chest. She'd kept her nails so pretty when she was engaged, eager to show off Derek's sizable ring, but the ranch work and simple neglect had made her hands look shoddy and inelegant. "I need the works," she said to the technician.

Dottie sat down in the next chair, admiring her own nails. "I'll probably go home to a mess of a house tonight with Ted watching the twins, but at least my nails will look nice." She gave Ellie a look. "I love the twins to bits, but they are a handful. The other day, when Jackson made me a rose out of clay, I thought my heart would melt, and then I laughed till I cried when Jason said the thing looked more like an octopus."

"You look really happy," Ellie offered, because it was true. Dottie had said she wanted to be a television newscaster in high school, and she was pretty enough to have had a shot at a media career. She'd never pursued it, though, opting instead for marriage right out of high school. Family life wasn't a wrong choice—Jackson and Jason looked to be adorable boys—but Dottie looked content in a way that felt nearly impossible to Ellie right now. "Motherhood agrees with you," she offered.

"It's exhausting, but, yeah. Those boys make me happy." Dottie leaned back. "I'm just glad I had twin boys while I'm young enough to keep up with 'em. Ted's talking about a third, but I don't know if I've got enough energy to be outnumbered like that."

Lydia, whom Ellie now realized was considerably pregnant, wiggled her toes in the pedicure chair. "Wayne says we're gonna have to shift to zone control when this one comes." Of course, Lydia had married Martins Gap's star quarterback Wayne Jacobs. Tiny little Lydia expecting her third child—Ellie could hardly get her mind around the idea. Sure, Martins Gap felt as if it hadn't changed, but the people in it sure had.

Only, *had* they? Or had they just continued along the expected track she'd fought to avoid? She'd gone off in search of a career and found one. She had done really well for someone only a year out of college. She had nice clothes, a sleek portfolio of public relations campaigns and a good apartment. She had professional prospects. She'd eaten food from all over the world and had even met celebrities.

And been cheated on by your fiancé with your best

friend, her heart reminded her with a surge of ice to her veins. How long would it be before that black spot would stop wiping out five years of achievements and adventures? It didn't seem fair that Derek and Katie could steal so much of her confidence and the pride she used to feel for the life she'd built when she wasn't the one who had done anything wrong. Why weren't *they* the ones hurting and running home? Why did it still feel as though they'd won and she'd lost when *they* were the cheaters?

"Bright red, please," Ellie declared to the technician.

"There you go!" called Wylene as she opened a box of blondies from Lolly's and began setting them on a cake plate. "You shout your fine self to the world, honey." She pointed to the technician. "What's the name of that new color came in last week, Jean?"

Jean reached behind her to pull out a bottle of very bright red nail polish and held it up to squint at the label. "Damsel Undistressed."

"That's the one for you," Wylene called. "And maybe get one of them bitty rhinestones on your ring finger. You know, just for a little extra oomph to make up for what ain't there no more."

Ellie didn't think she had to go that far. She'd had enough of shiny things on ring fingers for a while. "Just the red polish, please. Skip the bling for now."

Wylene slid a napkin topped with a large blondie on the counter next to Ellie. It had a bright pink fork stuck in the top. "I find the fork makes it easier to eat one-handed. No chance of ruining Jean's good work that way."

The tiny bit of consideration sparked a welcome warm glow in Ellie's heart. "Thanks, Wylene."

"Tell us about your big-city career, Ellie. It has to be exciting." Lydia shifted in her chair, one hand on her bulging belly. "I could use a dose of the good kind of exciting, not the 'Mom, Billy just ate a spider' kind of exciting."

Ellie's Atlanta life felt hectic and crazed, but she supposed it would appear exciting by Martins Gap standards. She allowed herself a tiny pleasure at the admiration in Lydia's voice. Back in school, how often had she looked at cheerleader-perfect-prom-queen Lydia and her handsome prom-king-quarterback boyfriend and envied their lives? What passed for important had been so different back then. It made her want to gather the knitting girls and find a way to make them understand how real life wasn't anything like high school.

"Do you go to lots of elegant parties? Ones with celebrities?" another woman asked.

"Sometimes," Ellie replied. "Although sometimes when you meet the celebrities, they don't end up being nearly as nice or glamorous as what you expected." Ellie told the story of the swanky singer known for his velvety romantic voice who turned out to be a mean, demeaning boor in person. "I went home and threw out all of his CDs," she told the wide-eyed group of women. "Our janitor is more of a gentleman than he is."

Just to balance things out, Ellie told the story of the beautiful woman who played everyone's favorite meanie on a popular soap opera. "She was even more beautiful in person. And she was so nice. Not a thing like her character. She sent a huge basket of muffins to the office after her party to say thank-you. Turns out, she's only a witch when the camera's on."

Everyone laughed, and Ellie felt the knots in her chest start to loosen. Maybe tonight wasn't such a mistake after all. Maybe reconnecting with these women she'd known as girls wouldn't be as difficult as she'd imagined.

By the end of the night, Ellie had gained more than pretty fingers; she'd gained a few new old friends. And that was the best pampering of all.

At the second garage session, Nash noticed that one of the boys—Mick—came to the church garage an hour early for the after-school program and was the last to leave. That Friday, Nash had noticed Mick repeatedly passing by the sheriff's office on a bicycle. Saturday morning, Nash looked up from sweeping out his house garage and caught sight of Mick leaning against a fence across the street. The boy was trying hard not to look as though he was watching Nash, but it was easy to see. Mick's body language told a familiar tale—he wanted to come over, yearned to connect, but wasn't quite ready to take the leap of being friendly with a lawman.

This was the open door, the foothold into a kid's life that used to get Nash so excited. Back in LA, it meant that all the time and energy he was pouring into troubled kids was finally taking hold.

Don't go back there, a corner of Nash's heart shouted in warning. *You're not ready to get into this again.*

Nash went back to sweeping for another five minutes but ended up stealing another look at Mick and the conflict in his eyes. The kid wanted to talk—needed to talk—but couldn't bring himself to come launch a conversation. Nash knew that look. He knew exactly the opportunity that look presented.

Nash's fingers tightened their grip on the broom, resistance warring with a call he knew would never truly disappear. Yes, he could stay safe and just deal with the kids as a group. It would do a little bit to help. Or he could risk going deeper and truly connecting with these young men. Put himself on the line and risk ending up hurt…again.

It surprised him how fast his old life—the burden to help, from which he now carried scars—sucked him back in. Was this who he was? Would always be? He could choose not to dive in. Then again, the way his gut reacted to Mick's cautious eyes and his hard-set shoulders, did he have a choice?

You could choose to be selfish. No one would blame you for protecting yourself after what you've been through, his sensible side argued.

And do this halfway? His other side retaliated. These kids' lives were filled with people who cared *halfway*. Teachers, neighbors and even parents who knew *of* them but didn't *know* them. The urge to help hadn't gone because the gift of helping hadn't gone. Whether Nash chose to recognize it or not, his heart still carried a burden for kids such as Mick. Besides, hadn't he already made that decision in some ways when he'd said yes to working with these kids?

Nash felt his new life slip a bit from his careful grasp as he put down the broom. He walked over to the small refrigerator set up beyond the tool bench. Out of force of habit—or was it something else?—he'd stocked it with a variety of sodas, as it had been in LA. Back in California, kids came to his garage "for a drink," but always stayed for much more. He would be opening up more than his garage to Mick if he walked across that street. Nash could shield himself from the pull of their lives and their stories as a group, but not one-on-one. The torn confusion in Mick's eyes gave him no choice.

Stay close, Lord, he prayed as he opened the fridge and took out two colas. *I still feel like I'm in over my head here.*

He opened both cans and walked across the street to where Mick stood trying to look as if he'd just happened to choose that particular fence to lean against. "Hey, there, Mick. Didn't see you till just now."

Actually, Mick had been there for half an hour, but Nash knew better than to call the boy out on that.

"You live here?" Mick acted surprised, as if it was pure happenstance that he was standing outside Nash's garage. It was almost amusing how the whole game came back to Nash with ease. Kids were never as unpredictable as everyone said.

Nash handed Mick the drink. "Got a minute? I need a hand with something."

Mick shrugged, paused to show a respectable amount of reluctance, then shrugged again. "I suppose."

"Good." Nash started back toward the garage, wracking his brain for a two-man job that could need doing just this minute. He settled on just letting Mick start the ignition and rev the engine up and down while he "checked" a few things under the hood. Simplistic, unnecessary, but it would give him the opening he needed. As they crossed into the garage, Nash fished in his pocket and tossed the keys to Mick. "Start her up, but don't put her in gear. You know how to drive stick?"

"Well, yeah." Mick said it as if Nash had just asked him if he knew how to breathe. "Doesn't everyone?"

"Not these days." Nash opened the hood as Mick got in the car—but not before Nash plucked the soda from his hand. "No open drinks in my baby." Mick rolled his eyes as Nash set the pair of cans down on the workbench.

They went through a series of "tests"—Mick revving the car at various levels while Nash pretended to fiddle with engine parts. The car was running fine, but Nash made sure to call out things like "Finally!" and "Glad that's working now." After a sufficient number of trials Nash leaned around the hood and called, "Shut her down." It did not surprise him that Mick got in one final roar of the engine before killing the ignition—it was a pretty sound to the right pair of ears.

"Do you know the firing order for an engine like this?"

Mick came around to stand beside Nash over the engine. "You mean like the spark plugs?"

"Exactly." Nash pointed to the distributor cap with the six spark plugs underneath.

Mick hovered his finger over the six plugs. "Um…1, 2, 3, 4, 5, 6?"

Nash swallowed a laugh at the novice assumption. "Nope. It's 1, 5, 3, 6, 2, 4," he said, hopping his finger across the line of plugs to show the alternating pattern. "That's why you need to read the repair manual before you just dive in. Lots of it you can do by instinct, but sometimes you need to get the right information or you just end up stumped."

"Well, it's a foreign car. Nobody I know drives an import."

Nash had heard some version of such sentiment before. "Maybe, but reading the manual is good no matter what you drive. What do you drive?" He already knew the answer to this question, but wanted to hear Mick admit his Chevy wasn't running at the moment.

"A hunk-of-metal Chevy that don't run right now."

"So let's change that. Sometimes you've just got to work with the car you have. Me, I like Datsuns—well, now they're Nissans, but you get the picture. I drove a Chevy myself for years before I could afford this car. Sturdy stuff. I learned the ropes on a Chevy. You can, too. It'll be good practice for you, and if money is tight, working on your own car can be a very good thing." Nash took a long drink. "Besides, if you see a pretty girl stuck by the road, you can stop and help her and be a hero."

"You know, that's how I started dating Marny." Mick took a long swig of his own drink. "She got a flat tire out by the highway, and I stopped and helped her change it."

Nash kept his tone casual. "So you and Marny, huh?"

A flush of teen infatuation filled Mick's features. "Yeah. She's…" He ran his hands through his hair—a gesture so close to what Nash had done thinking of Ellie that it made his breath hitch. "Well...amazing, you know?"

Nash handed Mick some greasy socket wrenches and a rag, then picked up one himself. Kids talked more openly while doing something else. He settled on one stool while Mick settled on the other. "How long have you two been a thing?"

"Since February. That's when her tire blew out. My car was still running then." Mick looked down. "Now we mostly take her car."

Ouch. Nash could feel the dent in Mick's pride. "So we should get your Chevy up and running. Do you know what she needs?"

Mick rolled his eyes. "What does every car need? What does every girl need? Money. Two more shifts down at Shorty's Pizza and I'll have the forty dollars more I need to buy the parts."

Nash remembered those days. In high school he'd had a coffee can in a dresser drawer that he'd stuffed with cash from his lawn-mowing business until he had enough funds for whatever part his car needed next. Twenty bucks had felt like twenty miles back then. "How about your folks? Will they help?"

Mick finished wiping one wrench and picked up the next. "Mom wants me to save up for tech classes at the community college. She still thinks you can do high school on a bicycle." He made a face that clearly showed his disagreement with that premise.

Nash had to agree. "Hard to date on a bicycle. And your dad?"

"Dad likes cars, but since he's been out of work he don't pay much attention to anyone. I think he and Mom are splitting soon. They think I can't tell, but come on. I'd have to be blind. Marny's folks split up right after her dad lost his job. We're just hoping her mom doesn't make her move to Waco once school's out."

That was a lot for a boy his age to be handling on top of school. "Waco's not that far."

Mick groaned. "It is without a car."

Nash took another long drink. He thought about what it had been like to zoom down the road with Ellie beside him, her hair flying every which way. And then he thought about how it would feel to be denied the freedom of the open road. His heart pinched in on itself, and he had to tell his hand not to reach for the pair of twenty-dollar bills sitting in his wallet. "When you finish those shifts, give me a call. I'll come over and help get you up and running."

He saw it then. That startled look kids got when they realized someone actually gave a hoot about how life felt for them. Lots of teens expected the world to love them, practically walked around demanding it. But some kids? They seemed to forget anyone even ought to notice.

"Yeah," Mick said, the hint of a smile crossing his usually sour face. "Okay, I will."

Chapter Ten

On the third week of the after-school program, as they drove to the Blue Thorn Ranch, Jose leaned his head out the window of the church van like a dog and said, "This is dumb."

Nash was amazed they'd gotten to the Blue Thorn entrance before one of the boys made a crack like that. The wave of derisive eye rolling that had met his announcement last week could have knocked a lesser man flat.

"It's not dumb," he replied, glad Ellie couldn't hear Jose. "And keep thoughts like that to yourself once we get on the ranch. The Blue Thorn means a lot to the Buckton family, and they and the girls need our help. You're going to learn a bit about what they're doing, and then you're going to teach the girls how to change a spark plug. A cultural exchange of sorts."

"I'd like to exchange a few things with Caroline Ivers, that's for sure," Billy said as he nudged Jose's shoulder.

"You keep that to yourself, too. And your hands, your words, probably even your eyes." Most of the girls in Ellie's class were a quiet kind of pretty—not the popular, decked-out kind of pretty, but sweet and clean even if rough around the edges. If only these boys could learn now that what made a girl stand out in high school could easily lose its charm out in the adult world. Still, he couldn't complain. He'd used the chance to hang out with the girls as leverage to get the boys to agree to this little adventure Ellie had dreamed up, anyway. "There they are—they beat us here."

Ellie stood next to Gunner's minivan with the girls from her class. He was glad to see that both the boys and the girls had followed directions and worn boots and long pants. Even though it was a warm April day, Ellie had explained to him that those things were necessary out in the pastures where they were going.

The boys piled out of the church van to stand in a posturing clump opposite the girls.

"Hello, boys," Ellie said cheerfully.

"Hi," Leon murmured.

Nash cleared his throat loudly and glared at the boys.

"Good afternoon, Miss Ellie," they said in reluctant unison.

Ellie raised an eyebrow at Nash, clearly surprised and not a little impressed. Nash felt a pleasant pang in his stomach that his first goal for the day had just been met. The stereotype of the well-mannered Southern boy evidently hadn't caught on with his current students. Not yet, anyway, but he was out to change that if he could.

"Miss Ellie," Nash began, "why don't you explain to everyone what it is we're doing today." Ellie had explained it to him, but he still found the whole thing odd and rather amusing.

"Sure," Ellie replied. "Everyone come over here and I'll show you."

She walked them over to the side of the barn. Leaning up against it was something that looked like a telephone pole with a set of giant street brooms attached lengthwise—as if someone had taken the roller brush out of a vacuum cleaner attachment and blown it up to twenty times its normal size.

"It's springtime, and the bison want to get rid of their winter undercoat. That's a good thing, because that downy undercoat is exactly what we want. It'll shed off naturally eventually, but it's much better for us—and for them—if they brush it off themselves."

"Can't you just cut it off, like my mom does to our sheepdog every summer?" the tallest of the girls asked with a giggle.

"You can't, Lucy. Or, more precisely, you shouldn't." Ellie looked at the boys. "Would any of you want the job of shearing one ton of angry-to-be-cooped-up bison?"

"No, ma'am," Leon piped up immediately. Skinny as he was, Nash guessed Leon would be snapped like a twig by even the smallest of the bison. Good. It might help his law-enforcement work if the boys were to realize just how dangerous bison were, and why it was such a bad idea for anybody to be taking potshots at the herd. They still hadn't solved the mystery of who was agitating the Blue Thorn herd, but Nash held to his conviction that the boys probably knew whoever was in on the stunt. Raising their awareness to the dangers of messing with the animals was the other reason he'd agreed to today's field trip.

"Exactly. Both you and the bison would end up hurt. And, trust me, you'd get the worst of it," Ellie said. "So instead of us shearing them, we give them the tools to do it themselves."

"You mean…?" Marny pointed to the brush.

"Yes," Ellie finished for her. "You're looking at a bison hairbrush. There are six of them stationed around the pastures, and we're going to go out and collect the down and hair off them."

"Eww. I bet it smells." One girl wrinkled her nose.

"It's a lot less messy than some of the other jobs around here, Ina Jean. And no, bison hair doesn't smell at all. Here." Ellie produced a patch of matted brown hair she had sitting on the fencepost. "It smells sweet, actually."

No one believed that, not even Nash, until Davey grabbed it and took a big dramatic sniff. His eyes popped. "She's right. My dog smells worse than this."

"I know *you* smell worse than that," Jose shot back.

"I'm still not as bad as you," Davey retorted, causing Nash to step between them.

"Okay, okay, let's cut the chatter and get to work. Miss Ellie, exactly how do we get the hair off the brushes?"

"With these." Ellie hoisted a bucket of what looked like garden rakes with short handles. "You'll need to pair up, one holding the sack while the other combs the hair off the brush." Working in boy-girl pairs had been Ellie's idea, and it was a good one. Well, the boys clearly thought it was a stellar concept. The girls didn't look quite so sure. To be fair, Nash's band of "car guys" wasn't especially smooth from a social standpoint. The idea here was for the task to be educational on a couple levels—agricultural and social.

"Like this." Nash didn't know much about the process, but Ellie had at least told him all the boys had to do was hold the bags. He took a bag from one of the sets of buckets and walked up to one side of the pole of brushes. Ellie proceeded to pull great hunks of brown fur—some long and hairy, some short and downy, just like the names she'd mentioned—from the massive bristles. Nash turned to the boys. "You guys can handle something this easy, right?"

"Sure." The guys huffed as if sack-holding were beneath their awesome skill sets.

"We'll leave the raking to the girls." Ellie's voice took on a teasing, almost flirtatious quality. "It requires a certain touch not to damage the fibers." Ellie winked at Nash, and the light little flutter of her eyelashes seemed to tickle the bottom of his stomach.

"Naturally," another of the girls said. "Guys never know what to do with hair."

Nash had the rebellious thought that he'd know exactly the right touch to handle Ellie's honey-colored waves. Ellie, in those faded jeans that hugged her curves, those long legs that ended in scuffed boots and those tawny cheeks that didn't need makeup, was real. Real in a way he'd never have expected to attract him. The fact that she wasn't even trying made it all the more powerful. Maybe the boy-girl pairing wasn't the smartest idea for this. If the adults were having a bit of trouble with distraction, how would the raging hormonal teenagers keep their focus?

As if to prove his point, Billy crowed as he stepped toward Ina Jean, "Oh, I know what to do with a girl's hair, baby. Let me show you."

"Show me you can get *the job done*." Nash stepped between them and thrust a bucket and sack into Billy's hands. "There's pizza and Grannie Buckton's world-famous brownies in it for you afterward." Adele Buckton had offered to feed the teens dinner so that the whole outing turned into a small party. Again, Nash felt it was good to get the kids meeting the Buckton family. If the person taking shots at the bison was among his teens, or friends of his teens, seeing the Bucktons as real people might make it harder to commit a mindless crime against their property.

Ellie pointed toward the pickup parked on the far side of the barn. "The herd has been moved to the north pasture out of our way while we work. You don't just wander around with the herd nearby. Bison aren't people-friendly."

"What about that one?" Doug asked. There was one bison in a smaller pen right up near the barn and house.

"That's Daisy. She was orphaned and bottle-fed as a calf, so she was raised around humans. I can let you meet her later on, but even Daisy has to be approached with care. One thousand pounds of animal is nothing to trifle with."

And nothing to shoot at, Nash thought as he motioned the teens toward the back of the truck. "I'll call off your pairs as we go."

"Wait, we don't get to pick our own partners?" Davey moaned.

"What kind of fool do you take me for?" Nash said as he tipped Davey's hat off his head, catching it with his other hand before handing it back to the boy.

Don't be a fool for Ellie, Nash warned himself as he watched the way she sauntered toward the truck. *She's dangerous in her own right.*

"I wasn't sure that was going to work," Ellie said as she poured Nash another glass of lemonade. "But it worked fabulously. We got all the brushes cleaned in a third of the time it would take Gunner and I." She looked over at the collection of hair- and down-filled sacks now sitting in the back of the truck. "I reckon we've got more than five pounds there."

Nash laughed, clearly unimpressed at the low weight. They'd worked for four hours. "Five pounds? That's a bag of sugar."

He really didn't get how this worked. "That's five pounds of light, fluffy stuff, remember. Once we clean it up and process it, that's enough to make seven skeins of yarn. The whole herd will produce about twenty pounds in a season."

Again, he looked nonplussed. "Seems like a lot of work for seven hanks."

Ellie handed him the lemonade. "Until you remember

that each hank goes for seventy dollars. Some can go for up to ninety."

Nash's head shook. "Ninety dollars. For yarn. I can't believe it."

She pulled herself up to her full height, but even at her considerable five-nine she had to crane up to meet his eyes. "Ninety dollars for high-quality knitting fiber, yes. Don't tell me you don't understand the concept of paying for quality."

"I do, but, Ellie, you're gonna give it to kids."

"I'm gonna *invest* it in those young knitters, yes. And in the future of Blue Thorn Fibers." When he gave her a sideways look, she pointed at him. "And I'm sure you put some of your own money into what you're doing with those boys. To teach them how to do good work, you need to give them good materials. You didn't start them off with shoddy tools. Now, why would I?"

"My tools are a bit more practical than yours."

She glared at him. There was no way Nash hadn't sunk some of his own funds into the program just as she had. "Fess up, Natsuhito. You've dug into your own pockets just like I have."

"Okay, Theo's budget wasn't enough to do what I wanted with the boys. So, yeah, I kicked a little in."

He'd kicked in more than a little if her intuition was right. It wasn't as if these kids had funds to spare. Blue Thorn Ranch had seen hard times but kept afloat thanks to Gunner's commitment and ingenuity. By contrast, many families in Martins Gap had been scraping by for years. Half the kids in the program had one or even both parents out of work. It was why Blue Thorn's refusal to sell land to an Austin real estate developer had caused such a stir; the developer had convinced the local folks that the Ramble Acres development would bring in lots of jobs.

She had no doubt that Nash already knew all of this, and that the boys had told him. She admired how Nash talked—*really* talked—with those boys. He knew all about their lives and their challenges. He managed to see past the oversize bravado most of them displayed to see the doubting, searching young men underneath. Did he realize how totally committed he'd become to the program? Derek was totally committed to his work— but he did it for acclaim, for the praise and material rewards it brought. His dedication was self-serving and artistically indulgent. Nash's intensity served a higher purpose.

She was coming to admire a lot about him. Especially because she could see what it cost him to invest himself in these kids. Here she was still giving herself over to bitter pouting about Derek and men in general, personally and professionally stalled for who knew how long. But Nash? He'd been burned—badly— probably by someone just like Jose or Mick. Yet he was still putting himself out there.

She touched his shoulder. "You haven't lost it, you know."

"What?" He wiped a smudge of dirt off his shirt where Davey had mistakenly knocked him into a clump of weeds.

"Your gift. Your ability to connect with those boys

and see what they have to offer when everybody else has written them off."

Nash looked down at the smudge again, unable to meet her eyes. "Oh, I don't know."

"I do. I'm not sure I could do what you've done. I mean, look at me—I'm still a mess over Derek, a romantic disaster zone who had to bite her tongue to keep from telling those girls all men are jerks. You, you're doing that 'all in' thing you said made the difference with kids who can't be that much different than the one who put you in the hospital. And I can already see how it's making a difference. Trust me, you haven't lost your gift. In fact, I suspect it's even stronger for how it's been tested."

Nash shifted his weight uncomfortably and ran a hand across his chin. "Now you're starting to sound like Pastor Theo."

"Yeah? What did he say to you?"

Nash looked out over the picnic tables, smiling just as she was at the classic high school joking and flirting that was going on between what had come to be known as The Car Guys and The Yarn Gals.

"Oh, I asked him if I should tell the boys the story of how I got here, and he gave me some high-sounding speech about why I should."

Ellie thought she would agree with the good pastor on that point. "What'd he say?"

Nash's face reddened just a bit. "Pastorly stuff."

Now he was hedging, and she wasn't standing for it. She set down the pitcher of lemonade and moved to stand in front of him. "Pastorly stuff like what?"

"He said…. Well, he said they ought to hear it because it would show them how a strong man of faith lets adversity make him stronger."

Ellie could tell the compliment both unnerved Nash and affected him deeply. "He's right, Nash. These guys could learn a lot from you."

"I'm not so sure."

Ellie waited until Nash's gaze finally returned to her. "Well, I am. You're a rare kind of man, Nash. There aren't enough men like you in this world."

He held her gaze for a moment, then looked away over her shoulder at the kids. "You don't have to tell me the world's mostly full of Dereks. And what's-her-names."

"Katies? Friends who'll turn on you quick as you can blink?" Some days Ellie couldn't decide which betrayal hurt worse—Derek's betrayal of her heart or Katie's betrayal of her friendship. "Katie made me feel as if anybody I let close could just turn on me." She looked at Nash, stung by just what a walking wounded shell of a human she seemed to have become. "I don't like who I am right now. I'm sour and brittle and pretty useless. I hate what Derek and Katie have made me into, but I'm not sure I can fix it just yet."

His eyes held no judgment. "You should have seen me during my weeks in the hospital and rehab. Sour and brittle? You betcha. Walking wounded? That was me, literally and figuratively. I don't think Derek and Katie will win this one. You'll fix it. It'll just take time."

"Just time, huh?"

"Well, time, faith, grace and, in my case, a lot of sushi. Guys eat their feelings, too, you know."

She laughed at that. "A sushi binge? Can't quite picture that."

He wiggled his fingers. "It involves a lot of octopus and eel. And rice."

She laughed harder and made a face. "Eww. I'll stick to Lolly's blondies. And Gran's brownies. And biscotti. And…well, you get the picture."

Nash cleared his throat. "Eel is vastly under-appreciated in the comfort-food market. You should look into it, professionally speaking." His serious words were totally undercut by the laughter in his tone and his eyes.

"No, thanks."

"No, really. Tell you what. You led me to barbecue. I'll lead you to sushi. Another long drive in the Z, because I'm reasonably sure we'll have to go to Austin for this."

The first meal had been spur-of-the-moment, a coincidental kind of thing. This felt like a bit more. She looked at Nash. "Are you…asking me out?"

Nash stepped back. "Of course not. I need to scope out Austin's decent sushi joints—for survival purposes and all—and it'd be more fun if I didn't have to do it alone." He held up his hands. "I'm not talking about anything even close to a date. This is more of a Support Your Local Sheriff campaign."

Ellie crossed her arms over her chest. "I saw that movie. It had James Garner, not raw sea creatures."

"Don't think of it as raw. Think of it as extremely fresh."

"So fresh it wiggled only hours before?"

"You're looking at this all wrong. Think of it as the first step in putting yourself back out there—a small act of courage between *friends*."

Ellie felt as if her courage had fled the county lately. Maybe sushi wasn't a bad place to start finding it again. "Okay. But no eel."

Chapter Eleven

Nash had just finished washing the last of the ranch mud off the church van when Pastor Theo walked across the parking lot from his home just west of the church. He pointed to the buckets and sponges at Nash's feet. "That's above and beyond the call of duty."

Squeezing out a sponge, Nash replied, "Car guys can't leave a car dirtier than when they found it. It'd have kept me up all night anyway, and I had some thinking to do."

That put a worried look on Theo's face. "The outing didn't go well?"

Nash dropped the sponge on the grass and began coiling the water hose he'd pulled from the garage. "No, it went great. Couldn't have gone better, actually."

"And so you're thinking about…?"

He knew he should have kept his remarks to himself. Pastors were too good at this sort of thing, asking probing questions and never leaving well enough alone. "Nothing."

Theo chuckled. "Hey, you don't have to tell me, but I will say that's the furthest nothing from 'nothing' I've heard in a while. Maybe you ought to talk about whatever it is."

Come to think about it, it might be a good idea to get Pastor Theo's help in keeping things within the right limits with Ellie. He needed someone to hold him accountable so that dumb ideas like sushi-exploration non-dates didn't happen again. Nash turned the empty bucket over and sat down on it. "It's not a whatever. It's a whoever."

Theo did the same with a second bucket. "I reckon those kids can be a handful."

Nash shook his head. "That's not exactly it." He ran his hands through his hair, finding it hard to even get the words out. He opted for quick and direct. "I lost my head and asked Ellie out today."

"Ellie Buckton? Yarn-gal-knitting-teacher Ellie?" Theo looked surprised, but not unpleasantly so. The man had a "happy consequence" look in his eyes that made Nash sorry he'd opened his mouth.

"Well, yes, but I was thinking more about the just-been-cheated-on-by-her-fiancé-and-best-friend-and-is-heading-back-to-Atlanta-someday-soon Ellie. I was able to stop and rephrase it to just a friendly outing when my brain kicked back into gear, but when I first brought up the idea of us having dinner, some part of me was asking her out."

Theo kicked a stone from the driveway. "And asking her out would be bad."

"Are you familiar with the term *rebound*, Theo?"

Theo had married his high school sweetheart, so Nash didn't think he had any idea what it was like to swim in the shark-infested waters of a dating pool like LA sported.

Theo scratched his chin. "Vaguely. And I do remember about a certain place having 'no fury like a woman scorned.' Only this is Ellie Buckton we're talking about. Stubborn? Maybe—she is a Buckton, after all. Fury and scorn? I'm not so sure."

"She told me she had to bite her tongue to keep from telling the girls all men are jerks. Even she admits she's a mess right now, and what woman in her spot wouldn't be? To find your fiancé getting all cozy with your best friend?"

"Oh, and you know nothing about what it feels like to be betrayed. You two have nothing in common." Theo pasted a mock-serious look on his face. "I can see where a date would be a problem. Good thing you caught yourself in time."

Nash returned Theo's sarcasm with the glower it deserved.

"Have you always been this serious about everything, Nash?"

Now, that wasn't a fair question. After what he'd been through, wasn't he entitled to think carefully about where he invested himself? And that was just the trouble—he was starting to be less careful. He was already caught up in rowdy kids and was in very real danger of getting caught up in a self-proclaimed "romantic disaster zone."

"Maybe" was the only answer he could give.

Theo put his hands in his pockets. "You and Ellie seem like you would make fine friends. Are you worried it could become something more?"

"It *shouldn't* become anything more."

"Not even if she might want it to?"

"That's just it, Theo. She's in a weird place right now. That Derek guy was a total jerk to her, so now anyone who treats her halfway nice is going to look like Prince Charming."

"And you're no Prince Charming?"

Nash sat up straight. "I'm a stand-up guy. But that's the problem. I have to tamp down this urge to treat her like she deserves, because that could just fire things up between us, and that can't happen."

"That can't happen," Theo repeated. "Because she's on the rebound and she's leaving."

Wasn't it obvious? Nash got up and began to collect the wet towels from around the car. "I'm not up for that. I'm thinking I'm probably not up for anything like a relationship for a while. Sure, I haven't come off some big breakup, but I've still got a lot of things to sort out."

"Well, if all that's true, what made you ask her out in the first place?"

"She got all mushy on me. Came at me with the same sort of stuff you said about not having lost my gift and how she was impressed with my courage with the guys' stuff. It got to me, and next thing I know I'm asking her out for octopus."

Theo gave him a quizzical look.

"Sushi," he explained as he worked, agitation overtaking him. "Suddenly I don't just want decent sushi, I want sushi with *her.* My brain goes out the window and I ask. I don't even realize it's coming out of my mouth. And then she balks and says, 'Are you…asking me out?' And my sense slams back into gear and I backpedal about friends and Support Your Local Sheriff, and… Well, it was a mess." Nash tossed the collected towels into the bucket he'd been sitting on. "So, yes, I have a little thinking to do."

Theo re-righted the bucket he'd been sitting on and began to toss the sponges into it. "Can you go out for—" he hesitated an absurd second before saying "—octopus and keep it friendly with Ellie?"

"I don't see where I have any choice. I told her dinner would be just as friends. If I back out now, I'll look like just another jerk of a guy." He looked at Theo, grateful to have someone with whom he could talk this through. Loner by nature that he was, he hadn't really felt a lack of friends. He had plenty of friendly citizen associates and coworkers, but not many real friends—until this moment. Surely that was part of the reason Ellie had gotten under his skin so fast. "I'm pretty sure I can keep this on a friendly basis. I just can't let her…get to me… like that again." He found one last towel and wrung it out. "But honestly, Rev, the color of those eyes ought to be illegal."

Theo laughed again. "Ah, the legend of the Buckton blues. I wasn't in town at the time, but I imagine my secretary, Dottie, could tell you stories of how Gunner Jr. and his brother, Luke, knew how to use those blue eyes to their advantage. And I suppose Gunner's wife could back you up on the power of those eyes. If it helps,

I agree you need to be careful with her. Ellie is a dear girl in a very vulnerable spot."

"No kidding."

"At the same time, I find myself thankful it is *you* she is turning to and not someone who might take advantage of that vulnerability. Better you taking care of her now than someone who will just hurt her more."

Nash hadn't thought of it that way. He could keep Ellie safe from someone who would stomp on her already tender heart. "If I just keep in mind that she's leaving soon, I could pull this off. We are working really well together on this project."

"The after-school program is going far better than I had ever hoped. You two make a great team. And you strike me as very capable of proving to her that not all guys are jerks. In fact, I can't help thinking our young men could learn a lot from watching you treat a pretty lady with respect and kindness, rather than… Well, you know."

He did know. Boys that age often had brains stuck in one gear, and it was not one associated with gentlemanly behavior. It wouldn't hurt to teach them how to tune up their social conduct alongside how to tune up transmissions. "Okay, so maybe my inviting Ellie to dinner wasn't the blunder I thought it was." He walked over to Theo, extending a friendly hand. "I've got a better handle on it now. Thanks for helping me think through this."

"I'm not sure I did that much, but I'm glad to help. I'd like to think you and Ellie are getting something out of this program for yourselves, too. Most times when I sink myself in a project, I find I get more out of it than all I think I'm putting into it. God's economy is pretty amazing that way."

"I hope that's true."

"For what it's worth, I really do think you haven't lost your knack with youth. I never have thought God's gifts come with expiration dates. But don't be inviting me out for octopus anytime soon, okay?"

Nash was glad to feel a laugh come easily. "Deal."

Saturday morning, Ellie showed her niece the layers of soft brown stacked up on the worktable. The down and hair the teens had collected had been washed and combed out and processed into fluffy sheets aptly called clouds. Normally the process took a long time, but a local mill had had an immediate slot open when she'd called. It felt like a little slice of encouragement from God. "Here they are, ready for spinning."

Audie touched the soft layers. "How'd it get so fluffy?"

"The place I sent it to washed it and combed it on a giant round brush. It's called carding, and it lines up all the hairs so they lay nice like this. Next I'll take it to another place, and they'll spin it up to become hanks of yarn."

"How?"

"Well, it's a big mill, so they use big machines, but…" Ellie wracked her brain to try to remember if she'd left a drop spindle somewhere on the ranch. Yes, there should be one in Gran's chest of yarn and fabrics that she stored in the guesthouse. "You know what? I can show you. Come with me."

Ellie grabbed the keys to the guesthouse from their hook in the kitchen and together they walked there. Audie stopped before the front door, little shoulders pulled back in pride. "This is where we lived before Gunnerdad and Mom got married, you know."

Working the key in the lock, Ellie gave her niece a broad smile. "I sure do. And I sure am glad you're part of our family now. It's really nice to see my brother so happy to be Gunnerdad." Every time Ellie said the inventive nickname, her heart glowed in true happiness for Gunner—and cinched a bit in sorrow for the happily married life that was not to be hers, at least not yet.

They made their way to the spare closet in the back room. Audie's eyes popped wide at all the treasures and trinkets stashed away—ribbons, fabrics, yarn, some old pieces of china, picture frames—countless remnants of the three generations of Bucktons who'd lived on the ranch. "I used to come here all the time when I was not much older than you, picking out things to put together and make new things." She squatted down next to Audie, who was running her hands over a stack of linen handkerchiefs, all embroidered with a big blue *B*. "Gran made those for my grandfather. Aren't they beautiful?"

"Pretty," the girl said. She looked at the materials with the same fascination Ellie had bore at her age. The kinship of creative minds bloomed warm and wide between them.

"You know, you can use anything in this chest you like to make things, but you have to ask Gran or me first." She pulled out a silver picture frame. "Some things are too precious to use any old way." Turning the old gray-brown photo toward Audie, she explained, "Look here. This is Gran when she was a new bride. And that's my and Gunnerdad's grandfather."

Audie's nose wrinkled. "Why aren't they smiling? Mom and Gunnerdad are smiling all over the place in our photos from the wedding."

Ellie had given the same reaction when she had first seen the photograph. "Back then, people had to look serious in their photos. It looks kind of funny to us now, doesn't it?"

"Sure does."

"But I can tell you, Gran and Grandad were happy. As happy as your mom and Gunnerdad are now." *As happy as I wanted to be.*

Audie sat back on her heels. "You're not getting married anymore, are you?"

That was Audie: direct as an arrow and just as fearless. "No, sweetie, I'm not."

"Are you really sad?"

Ellie swallowed back the huge lump that rose in her throat. She didn't want to get into the ravages of unfaithfulness with a nine-year-old, but it would also be wrong to gloss over what had happened. "I am. The man I was going to marry did something that hurt my heart very much. And you should never marry someone who thinks it's okay to hurt you that deeply." She took a deep breath and returned to digging through the closet. "So, while I'm really sad right now, I think it was the right choice. And I'm trying to trust that out there somewhere, God has the perfect guy for me just waiting."

"Mom tells me God had Gunnerdad waiting for her when she was ready. We were both really sad when my daddy died. So if we can be happy again, I think you can be, too."

Wise, wise words from someone so young. Ellie hugged her niece. "Thank you, darlin'. That feels really good to hear. Sometimes the right choices hurt, and it's good to have friends beside you to say things like what you just said to me."

"Gunnerdad says someone is shooting at our bison. I love our herd. Hurting them isn't a right choice at all. I'm mad at whoever is doing that. It's wrong."

Ellie stopped rummaging. "It is. And I'm mad at whoever is doing it, too. And when I'm mad or sad, I knit. Or make something. Or bake and eat too much of it."

Audie scrunched up her face. "Is that why we're in here? Looking for something to make?"

Ellie laughed—the wet, laughing-through-tears kind of laugh that was her best source of healing these days—and poked Audie on the nose. "Sort of. We're looking for my drop spindle so I can show you how to make yarn. We'll send most of it to the big machines, but the best part is that we can get started right now. And this is so easy, even you can do it. *Aha!* Here it is." She pulled out the polished wooden spindle she'd received as a Christmas present when she was fourteen. "I'm going to teach you how to use this because I want you to have it."

"Really?"

Another young knitter born into the craft. Ellie's heart lifted a little bit more. "Absolutely, kiddo. You know, some of the hair and down in those clouds probably belongs to Russet." Gunner had let Audie pick the name for Daisy's calf all those months ago, before he and Brooke even started dating. Though Gunner had secretly feared Audie would come up with something absurdly girlie like Rainbow Sparkle, she'd risen to the occasion. "You gave Russet his name. Now he can give yarn back to you."

Audie grinned. "I like that."

"Me, too. Come on. Let's go on back to the big house and get started."

Ellie got up to leave, but then turned back. Looking at the photo of Gran and Grandad—so serious, yet she knew them to be so happy. She scooped up the photo to take back to her room, deciding to put it on her dresser as a reminder. *I come from a family of love. Love will find me again even though I'm frowning now. Right, Lord? Help me remember that.*

They sat on the ranch-house porch as Ellie showed Audie the simple techniques in drop spinning. Stretch out the fibers with two fingers, spin the spindle, let the fibers twist around to become yarn—it really was easy enough for someone Audie's age, and she took to it as if she'd been doing it all her life.

"At this rate, you'll have enough to knit booties for your new little brother by the time he's born."

"You're a good teacher, Aunt Ellie. This is fun."

Audie's enthusiasm was nothing short of a gift. Any

lingering doubts Ellie had about success with the after-school class fell away in the sparks of excitement in Audie's eyes. This was part of Ellie's talent. Nothing gave her a charge of energy like introducing someone to the joy of knitting. Watching Audie stare intently as she twisted the fuzzy roving through her fingers and let the weight of the spindle stretch the twists out into strands, Ellie saw the same zing of creativity capture her niece that had once captured her. It hadn't been a mistake to run home to the ranch. This truly was the best medicine for her heartache, and God had laid the opportunity before her as the balm she needed.

"Are you gonna teach those girls how to do this?" Audie asked.

"Maybe. And I'll be thrilled if they take to it as well as you have. I've started them off on knitting with store-bought cotton yarn, but once the mill has processed all the down and hairs they gathered off the brushes, each girl will get back her very own hank of Blue Thorn bison yarn."

"But I'd rather make it into yarn myself like this. Do I really have time to make something for our new baby?"

Audie's eyes were so sweet and eager. "Yes, but if you want it done by the time he's born, it should be something very small like booties or mitts." Ellie couldn't help but add, "Your baby brother is going to be very blessed to have a big sister like you." She helped Audie graft the next bit of fiber into the strand she was spinning, pleased at the way her niece was picking up speed. "Have your mom and Gunnerdad picked out a name for your brother yet?"

Audie laughed as if this were a ridiculous question. "Of course they have."

Ellie applied an exaggerated pout. "Well, nobody's told me." She had a good guess, of course, but it felt amusing to give Audie the chance to proclaim the news.

"They shouldn't have to. Everybody knows his name's gonna be Gunner Buckton III. Gunnerdad says we're gonna call him Trey for short. I like that nickname. Baby Trey. Don't you like it?"

Ellie felt the idea of a fourth generation of Bucktons on the ranch settle warm and glowing around her. "I like it very much. I like it so much I think Trey should have booties *and* mitts. I'll help you with the spinning so you have enough yarn, okay? We're family. We should help each other out."

Audie grinned. "Then can I make something for Gran? She's always making stuff for me."

The girl had such a sweet heart. It was easy to see how she'd charmed her way into Gunner's life and softened him the way she had. "I know Gran would just love that. It's always a good idea to make things for the people who love you."

"Are you always making something for someone who loves you?" Audie's eyes popped wide with dismay when she realized that might not have been a good question. Still, she loved the girl's constant curiosity.

Ellie sighed, thinking about the unwound shawl for Katie sitting awaiting its transformation in a corner of her room. "I was. I had a very pretty shawl in the works that my best friend was going to wear in my wedding."

The words stung, but she didn't choke on them the way she'd expected.

Audie continued her spinning as she talked. "But you're not anymore?"

How to explain this very adult situation to a child? "Well, we're not best friends anymore. I'm really sad about that, too."

"That's sad. My best friend and I had a fight last month, and it was all I could think about."

That's about the way it goes, Ellie thought. "Sure is."

"What about Mr. Derek? Did you knit things for him?"

Ellie sat back in her chair. "Now, there's a funny thing about that. Some knitters say knitting something for your boyfriend—a sweater most especially—will doom the relationship. A silly superstition, you know. Even so, I never did knit anything for Mr. Derek—and look what happened. Just goes to show you that paying attention to silly superstitions is…well…silly."

Audie leaned against Ellie while she kept spinning. "Boys can be dumb. Derek must be dumb, 'cause I think you're the nicest person ever."

The pint-size declaration of loyalty set a glow in Ellie's chest that was worth a dozen perfectly knitted shawls. "Thanks, kiddo. I feel the same way about you."

Chapter Twelve

Nash pushed the button on the Blue Thorn Ranch gate. He'd been called to come over Sunday morning even before he could get to the church service in town. "It's Nash Larson from the sheriff's office. I came as quickly as I could."

Adele Buckton's voice crackled over the speaker. "Oh, Deputy Larson, I'm glad you could get here so fast. Everyone else is out by the barn, so go straight there. I can't believe someone would do this to one of our animals. I'm just sick about it."

"We'll get to the bottom of it, Mrs. Buckton. You have my word." Nash pulled the cruiser onto the ranch road before the gate was even fully opened. Nash was "on call" this morning, and the call from Gunner had come in not fifteen minutes ago. One of the ranch's bison had been found shot dead out on the far west side of the ranch. Things had officially moved up a notch from foolish nuisance to deliberate crime. While it felt like a nasty thing to hope for, Nash's job would be easier if the bullet was still lodged in the animal. If the ballistics matched what he and Gunner had found earlier, they'd have a better chance of catching whoever did this before he did any more harm to himself or the Bucktons' herd.

Billy Flatrock, the ranch foreman, met him outside the barn. "The carcass is in the back of a trailer out behind the barn. I'm trying to keep this away from little Audie. Brooke took her to church so she wouldn't see. If this creep had shot Russet, I don't know what Audie would do."

"Russet?" The Blue Thorn raised bison for meat as well as for conservation of the species. Surely they didn't go around naming the animals like pets, did they?

"Audie has a particular connection with one of last year's calves. It happens. Gunner's rather partial to Russet's mother, too. I wouldn't want any of the Blue Thorn herd to be hurt, but most especially that family."

Nash couldn't help but raise an eyebrow at the use of the word *family*. Flatrock caught his expression as they walked around the barn. "We preserve family groupings here, Deputy Larson. We honor the animals, even when we harvest them." The foreman stopped walking and looked Nash straight in the eye. "I take this shooting personally—very personally. Gunner even more so. We need this stopped."

"I agree. Have you called the vet? I'd want his opinion and his help retrieving any evidence that may still be in the carcass."

"I'm surprised he didn't beat you here. He should be along any minute."

Nash and Billy Flatrock turned the corner to see the large animal lying in the bed of an equipment trailer, the bloody wounds in its chest and shoulder exposed and drawing flies. His gut tightened at the injustice of it—taking down livestock for sport or spite wasn't just illegal, it was wrong and mean. If this was a kid, it was a kid heading fast in a bad direction.

Gunner walked up behind him, pocketing his cell phone. "A fine animal. She would have brought a high price next year. No sign of illness or anything else that might have separated her from the herd."

Nash pulled on a pair of latex gloves and walked closer. Even as a calf, the animal was huge. "Are you thinking whoever did this fired right into the herd?"

"I don't want to think anyone would be that foolish, risking a stampede, but yes, that's probably what happened. She wouldn't have been one of the slower ones, but she might have been on the edge of the herd. Larson, I don't like this one bit. There's more going on here than the loss of one animal."

Nash lowered his voice. "I agree we should look at this as an attack. Any idea if it's against you personally or the ranch?"

Gunner's eyes were as serious as his tone when he answered, "I have no idea."

He hated to ask this, but Nash felt as though he had no choice. "Do you think whoever is doing this might step things up? Threaten you or the family?" It was a terrible thought to put in an expectant father's head, but unpleasant warnings were part of the job.

"I pray not. And I've had no reason to think so up

until now." Gunner looked at the beast slumped in a brown furry mass in the trailer. "But this feels like a deliberate killing."

Nash shifted his weight as he turned to face the rolling pastures. "I have to say I agree. Can you shift the animals indoors?"

Gunner gave a dark "you don't come from around here, do you?" laugh and shook his head. "These are bison, man, not sheep. They're out in the open no matter what. Maybe we can pray for rain to keep whoever's shooting indoors, but aside from that, I don't know." The rancher stared hard at Nash. "You and Don need to find this guy, and fast."

Well, you told God you were bored, Nash chided himself as the pressure of the case settled hard on his shoulders. *Now you've got kids to teach and bison to save. A nice, full schedule.* He turned to see Ellie coming out of the big house. She walked toward Gunner, Billy and Nash as they stood huddled around the trailer and carcass.

"Gunner," she said as she grabbed her brother's hand. "How is this happening?" She looked up at Nash. "Hi, Nash. I can't believe this."

For the first time, Nash truly noticed how much alike Gunner and Ellie looked. Sure, the striking eyes were what everyone noticed, but the hair and the set of cheekbones declared them family. Being an only child himself, siblings held a fascination for him. To be part of a family of four children felt as foreign as the *y'alls* and *howdys* that filled his ears in Martins Gap. Ellie had mentioned two more siblings. Would the threat to the ranch bring those two home? Or could there be bad blood between estranged siblings that might lead to something like this? While he needed to consider every possibility, Nash's instincts still told him this was a prank orchestrated by some teens who had gone wrong. Buckton had every right to be concerned—this killing clearly took things up a notch—but that still didn't mean this couldn't be the result of a dare that had gotten out of control. For everyone's sake, Nash hoped that was true.

"Can you give me a list of ranch hands? Including anyone you've recently let go?"

"Sure. We're not big enough to have a year-round staff—it won't take long. Give Billy and me ten minutes to make up a list." With that, Gunner and Billy walked back to the house. That left Nash and Ellie staring at the doomed animal.

"This is wrong," Ellie said, resting her hand like a benediction on the large brown head with its lifeless eyes. "You shouldn't have died for no reason like this." Her voice was tight with sorrow and compassion for the animal. "What possible good can come of something like this? Why do it?"

"It is hard to see. Gunner said she would have gotten a good price—can't anything be salvaged? You can't still use the animal for meat if it's just died? I mean, I don't know how all this works, but to lose an animal like this…"

"Look. She was shot more than once. And in the wrong places. We don't harvest like that at Blue Thorn. We don't give the animals any reason to fear. Not only is it just plain wrong, but fear releases a hormone called cortisol into the bloodstream. It affects the meat—you can actually taste the difference." She turned away from the carcass. "Even if we could eat it, I don't think I could bring myself·to." The wind whipped her hair across her eyes and she reached up to push it back. "Such a senseless waste. What's the matter with the world that everyone thinks it's okay to hurt everyone else?"

"What about the fur? The hide? Does that cortisol hormone affect those things?" Nash felt as if it was a stupid suggestion, but there had to be some way to keep this from being a total loss. To lose the animal completely—both in life and in use—felt like giving the shooter too much of a victory.

Ellie blinked up at him. "No. Cortisol doesn't affect the hide." She ran her hand over the bison's head again. "We can shear and use hides from harvested animals, so it is possible. It's probably what Gunner will do— we can't just let an animal go to waste like this. Still, I don't think I could stomach using a murdered animal's coat for fiber or leather."

It did sound rather cruel. Then again, no less cruel than allowing the animal to just die as the result of a stupid prank. "I'm sorry. Maybe I shouldn't have suggested it. It was a dumb idea."

She squared her shoulders. "No, it's not." She looked back at the animal, as if asking its permission. "I mean it's a horrible situation, but what's the point in letting it stay horrible?" She gave Nash a long, pleading look and grabbed his hand. "Find who's doing this, Nash. Please."

Her hand felt warm and strong against his palm. The

urge to ease her pain, to protect her while she healed, surged up powerfully within him. "I will, Ellie. I will."

"Ellie?"

Ellie sank into the chair in Gunner's study that afternoon, reeling from the unexpected sound of Derek's voice. She didn't need to take this kind of hit today. "Why are you answering Pete's phone?" She'd set up a call on a Sunday specifically to avoid Derek, who was often too busy with Sunday brunch to be anywhere near the offices.

"I was in his office checking on something. I saw your name on the screen. I've tried every other way to talk to you, but you won't take my calls or reply to my messages."

Thanks, boss. Ellie would have a thing or two to say to Pete for letting Derek spring himself on her like that. She'd finally gathered up the nerve to discuss her work situation with her boss and he put Derek on the line? Ellie shut her eyes and forced all the strength she could into her voice. "I don't want to talk to you, Derek. You don't have anything to say that I'm interested in hearing."

"How about I'm sorry? I am. I really am, you know."

There was something deeply satisfying about hearing Derek finally apologize. But it also meant hearing that smooth, silky thing he did with his voice that could convince anyone to do anything. Derek was a fabulous cook, but he was an exquisite persuader. She brought up the vision of his hand running down Katie's arm to steel herself against his charm. She'd have to forgive him someday—sooner rather than later, if only for her own peace of mind so she wouldn't have to carry that anger around inside her—but she wasn't ready now. "Thank you. Now please let me talk to Pete."

"He stepped out of the office for a minute so I could talk to you. How are you? Are you in Texas? Pete said you took the vacation time you had saved up for the honeymoon and a leave on top of that. I'm worried about you. You didn't have to run away. We could have gotten past this."

At least Pete had kept his promise not to tell anyone exactly where she'd gone—not that Derek had looked very far, or he surely would have thought to call the ranch. *Past this?* There was no gentle way past this. There was only slogging through the wreckage—at least for her. Derek's voice sounded so calm and collected, so *unharmed.* As if it had cost him nothing to throw away their relationship, while Ellie felt as if it had cost her most of her sanity and all her confidence. Slog through that in the blinding gossip spotlight of Good-Eats? No thank you. "I had to get away for a while." *I'm sure you're loving being the center of a juicy gossip storm, but it's not my thing.* "It's not like I could have gotten any work done anyway." Truly, Ellie felt as if she'd left all her concentration and resolve back in Atlanta. She was used to being productive and focused, but these days she felt as if she wandered through time like twigs floating down the creek that ran through the back of the pastures.

"I really am worried about you, Ellie. Are you sure you're okay?"

Okay? She wasn't anything close to okay. How could Derek even think she was okay? She hadn't said anything of the sort. Her stomach tightened. "No, Derek, I'm not okay. I will be, but I'm not now." She rose out of the chair. "And that's on you. I suppose some small part of me is glad—or will be—that you cheated on me before I vowed to spend the rest of my life with you, but you still hurt me." Tears threatened, but she tamped them down. She would not fall apart in front of Derek. He didn't deserve to hear her in pieces. "So worry all you want. And don't call or pull a stunt like this again. Please put Pete on the phone now."

"Ellie." His voice was a perfect combination of smooth and sorrowful. He could always reduce her to puddles with the way he said her name.

She began pacing around the study. "I mean it, Derek. Don't make me hang up on you, because I will."

Ellie heard Derek mutter something, flinching with the clang of the receiver hitting Pete's desk. She heard faraway voices for a moment, then Pete picked up the phone and sighed. "So I blew that one. I shouldn't have given him the phone, but when he saw it was you... Well, I'm sorry. Bad call."

Pete was the best part about working for GoodEats. Demanding, certainly, but honest and fair. He worked long hours right alongside his staff and was quick to praise a job well done. "Please don't let him talk to me again. I'm not ready, okay?"

"He's been crazy since you left. Well, crazier than usual. Brilliant—he's done amazing things with the dessert menu—but wild and short-tempered. For what it's worth, you were good for him."

"Yeah, well, it turns out he wasn't so good for me." Ellie sat against the edge of Gunner's desk, fiddling with a coaster Audie had made. One of those kit projects made from jersey loops. She'd help Audie make dishcloths with cotton yarn next week, maybe. "No offense, but I'm glad I left. How's the intern working out taking up the slack?"

She could hear Pete sit back in his chair. "You won't like the answer."

While Ellie knew she'd left at an inopportune time, she also knew it had been the right choice to leave. "Not stepping up to the plate? She struck me as the ambitious type. I thought she'd dive right in."

"Oh, she has. But she doesn't have your knack. The media kits for the GoodArt gala are boring. You're going to need to do some first-class schmoozing when you get back."

She noticed he said "when," not "if," and her stomach tumbled in indecision about how to take that. The GoodEats GoodArt Fine Arts Gala was one of the special projects that Pete had brought her into as his direct assistant. It was a wildly successful fund-raiser for school visual arts, supporting a collection of programming that had fallen prey to the city's public school system budget crunch. Shortchanging the gala's advance publicity had been the hardest part about leaving Atlanta. Part of her hoped it would be the one thing that ensured her return— she just wasn't sure how large a part. "You managed before I came on board, you'll be okay without me." The words tasted dry and dismissive on her tongue.

"Yeah, we'll get by. But how are you? I mean, really, how arc you?"

Somehow the question dug so much deeper when Pete asked it. Ellie scrambled for the right response. "I'm a carefully controlled mess. Okay, maybe not so carefully controlled. I'm glad I'm here, and my family's being great, but it's like my brain forgot how to work."

"You're grieving."

She'd not thought of it that way, but Pete was right. A huge part of her life had just died. Had been put to death, actually, just like that bison out behind the barn. A whole slew of hopes and dreams snuffed out in the space of one heart-wrenching discovery. "I guess I am."

"Look, I know we talked about you coming back mid-May, and we'll get by if that's what you need, but I'd be lying if I said I wouldn't love you to come back sooner."

Ellie was one of dozens of smart people at GoodEats. Pete's plea hit some long-sore spot in her that had always wondered if anyone would really notice when she left. How sad that such an affirmation came in the midst of too much heartache to make it useful. "I don't know, Pete. I'd be of no use to you right now. Believe me." If half a dozen teenagers could practically reduce her to tears by not being thrilled with her class, how on earth would she meet Pete's high expectations for handling reporters and charity committees in this condition?

"Just think about it. Come back when you're ready, but get ready as fast as you can. We need you."

In her senior-year internship and her full-time job at GoodEats since graduating, Pete had never said anything so gratifying as those three words. Derek didn't need her love. Katie clearly didn't need her friendship. Gran and Gunner loved her, but they had their own lives and didn't need her. It felt deeply satisfying to be needed, even if it was only professionally. "Thanks for saying that, Pete. It helps a lot to hear it."

Pete laughed softly. "It would have helped you to hear what Miguel said to Derek when he heard what had happened."

Miguel was the head of housekeeping for the restaurants—a paunchy, pushy old man with a thick Mexican accent and a great big heart. Ellie had won his loyalty by getting a magazine to run a piece on the stellar health and safety record GoodEats enjoyed. She could just imagine the slew of chastisements Miguel sent Derek's way. "Really?"

"He went on for ten minutes. And while it was all in Spanish, believe me, no one needed a translation." After a pause he added, "We need you back, Ellie. I get that you're hurting, but I don't want to do the June gala without you on board. You love your work. Maybe getting busy again would be the best thing. I don't see you puttering around on the family ranch forever—you need to be busier than that."

"I'll think about it. I promise." If Pete saw what time Gunner rose in the morning and how tired he looked when he came in for dinner, he wouldn't use a word like *puttering* for ranch work. The Blue Thorn was a lot of work and if she chose to get busy, there'd be no end of tasks awaiting her here. It was just that she couldn't seem to get in gear. Pete's declaration of how important she was to the company was a balm to her soul. What she did at GoodEats mattered, and she'd needed to hear it.

So why did it have to take a disaster and a departure before she heard it?

Chapter Thirteen

❧

This is not a date. This is friends going out for dinner.

It bothered Nash how often he'd had to repeat it to himself as he drove to the ranch house Tuesday night. He wasn't used to picking up women with their whole family watching—it felt like high school prom. For one moment, when Ellie's little niece, Audie, skipped out of the house to make a big *ooh* face at his sports car, Nash considered asking her to come along. A nine-year-old chaperone? Was he that desperate for accountability? Had he completely forgotten the Z had only two seats?

"I like your car." Audie peered into his driver's side window with wide eyes as he shut off the engine. "It looks like a race car."

"It's not," he said as he stood up out of the low seat. "But it's close enough." He surprised himself by saying, "Would you like me to take you for a ride someday?"

"Sure!"

"Well, since you'd have to sit in the front seat and all, it'll take a little doing, and we'd definitely need your mom's okay. But maybe someday soon we can make that happen."

Ellie walked up looking…well…absolutely perfect. Not full-on date fancy, but clearly a step up from her normal everyday wardrobe. She wore a casual floaty yellow dress that made her eyes stand out even more than usual, and he smiled at the neon-green toenails that peeked out from flat sandals rather than dressy heels.

She noticed him looking—something that made Nash's stomach wiggle. "Audie did my pedicure yesterday. It's a bold color choice, don't you think?"

"Couldn't say. Definitely not my area of expertise."

Ellie leaned down to Audie. "Deputy Larson's area of expertise, the one he's going to show to me today, is sushi—that's raw fish."

"And some other things," Nash added.

"Gunnerdad said sushi's made with things like octopus. Those aren't fish. Those are cephalopods."

Nash felt his smile broaden at the little girl. "I didn't know that. You're very smart."

"Or at least very curious. And very talkative." Audie's pregnant mother, Brooke, waddled up behind her daughter. "Why don't we let Aunt Ellie and Mr. Nash get on their way."

"When you take me on my ride, can we go to eat octopus?"

Curious indeed. Even most teenagers would turn up their noses at the thought of eating octopus. "You're not scared to eat it?"

Audie's tiny chin went up. "I'm not scared to taste it. I'll only *eat* it if I like it."

"Well," said Nash as he opened the car door for Ellie. "I can't argue with that strategy."

Audie started to say something else, but Brooke tugged her away—but not before giving Ellie a look that was either "enjoy yourself" or "watch yourself," Nash couldn't say which.

"Gran says Audie's a hoot wrapped around a firecracker." Ellie laughed as the car turned out of the elaborate stone-and-iron Blue Thorn gate.

"Pretty fair description," Nash agreed. "Your family is nice."

"My family is nosy," Ellie corrected. "They all lined up on the porch as if this was prom."

Nash burst out laughing. "You know, I had the exact same thought." And then, because it needed saying, he added, "But it's not. This is just a fun dinner between friends. I'm not looking for anything else, Ellie, and I know you aren't, either." Sure, it was awkward, but it was best to keep that line clear and out in the open.

"Thanks. I love my family, but it sure feels good to have a night away from them. Everyone is always asking me how I'm feeling, have I decided what I'm doing next and quoting that 'all things work together for good' Bible verse." She let her head fall back against the seat as the wind played with her hair—a sight that tightened Nash's gut and made him glad he'd declared the platonic nature of the evening just now. Did this Derek idiot have any sense of what he'd thrown away?

"I know they mean well," Ellie went on. "But I'm feeling different every hour, I don't know what I'm going to do next and while I get that God hasn't played some horrible trick on me, some days I'm just plain hurt and angry. They probably think I hide on the porch and knit because I'm sad, but mostly I just hide on the porch and knit because I'm tired of talking about it."

That gave Nash an out, at least. "So, rule number one for tonight is I don't bring up your recent—" he searched for a kinder phrase than *getting dumped* "—social hurdles. But if you find you want to talk about it, bring it up. I can handle a mild round of ex-trashing." It would probably do him good to hear how Ellie was still broken up over Derek. A reminder that she was in the throes of romance rebound and off-limits.

"I decided to ban myself from Derek-bashing. I took a morning earlier this week and wrote a long, scathing letter to him, getting it all out of my system. I wrote one to Katie, too. Then I put the letters in the fire and declared that the end of it. Or at least to try to make that the end of it."

"I tried that tactic once. The police-force therapist had me write a long letter to Hector Forrio. I didn't burn it. I actually gave it to the therapist. She said she would give it to him in prison."

"Wow," Ellie said, turning to look at him. "Did it help?"

Nash was glad he was driving and didn't have to return her gaze. "Nope. Well, maybe for a week or so while I waited for a response from him. Of course, none came. I can't be even sure he ever read it. But did it take away the anger and all that? Not really. I think only time—and lots of it—can do that." *You remember*

*that, Larsen. She needs time, and neither of you have
got that before she'll be leaving again.*

"It's funny, you know?" Ellie stuck her hand out the
window. Out of the corner of his eye, Nash could watch
her play with the rushing wind the way a child would,
hand floating up and down. It struck him as exquisitely
pure, having the same simple and untarnished nature
that the rolling pasturelands gave off. The exact opposite
of LA's loud sheen.

"What?"

"Well, I was thinking about it. That kid was aiming
for your heart and missed. Derek wasn't even paying
attention to my heart and shot it right through. It's
funny."

"So we *are* going to talk about Derek?" He had been
sure her ban wouldn't last the night. Women as a whole
weren't able to compartmentalize this kind of stuff the
way men did. It was what made Ellie such a minefield
at the moment.

"That wasn't really about Derek. It was about why
you and I are friends. We're the odd opposite of each
other. Get it?"

"Sort of." *I get that it hurts*, he wanted to say. *But I
don't put someone trying to snuff you out in the same
column as getting cheated on. Even by a fianc*é. One
was a crime, the other a sad outcome. Still, she was in
the throes of it, and he nearly a year's healing under his
belt. "We both ran."

Her hand kept skimming and diving through the
darkening night air. "A pair of runaways." She shifted
to face him and the breeze sent cascades of tawny

hair across her cheeks. She didn't mind how the T-top messed with her hair—she seemed to enjoy the way it tumbled over her face. He liked that. "What's your favorite color?"

Nash had to think a moment—it had been years since anyone asked him a question like that. "Green."

"Why isn't your car green, then?"

"This car came in two color combinations, black and gold or black and red."

Ellie ran her hands over the gold of the door panel as though assessing whether he'd chosen the correct combination. "You couldn't just have painted it the green you liked?"

"No. That would devalue the car. The whole point of a classic car is to have it as close to the factory issue as possible. It's not like knitting a scarf—you don't just pick your favorite color." His words gave a sudden sense to her question. "Is that why you were asking? Were you going to knit me a scarf?"

Her face went the most disarming shade of pink. "Maybe," she admitted, and Nash's stomach did another somersault. "I knitted things for all my friends. You should have seen the shawl I was knitting for Katie to wear in the wedding. A work of art—that is before I ripped it all out with Gran on the porch the day after I came back. A very satisfying purge, if I do say so myself."

He shouldn't ask, but he couldn't stop himself. "What did you knit Derek?"

"Well, you'd have thought I'd knitted him a sweater the way things turned out."

"Meaning?"

"It's an old superstition knitters have. Knitting any-thing—but most especially a sweater—for a boyfriend dooms the relationship. Can't be too true if I never knitted a sweater for Derek and the whole thing blew up on me anyway, can it?"

Drawing the connections in his head, Nash concluded that if Ellie was considering knitting him a scarf, that meant she placed him squarely in the friend column of relationships. That ought to be good news, but it irritated him anyway.

They drove on in comfortable silence until Nash took the Austin exit and pointed at a row of buildings just down the street. "We're here."

"You know," said Ellie as she considered the peculiar texture of raw octopus, "it's not bad. I can't believe I'm saying this, but it's actually tasty. Weird, but satisfying."

Nash poured more soy sauce in the little china bowl beside his plate. "I think that's why I crave it. Nothing else tastes like it. I put soy sauce on lots of things, but sushi is a particular taste."

Ellie picked up some rice with her chopsticks—she'd eaten enough Chinese takeout in Atlanta to know how to use the utensils well. "Here in Texas we put hot sauce on everything. Still, I don't think it's the same. You'd never put this on breakfast eggs, but Gunner loads his with hot sauce."

"I've seen how you all douse your breakfast eggs with hot sauce," Nash offered. "I mean, I like the stuff, but only on certain things." He pointed to another piece of sushi on the large platter between them. "That one has tuna in it—a bit milder in taste than octopus. It goes together really well with that one over there." It was fun to see the mentor side of him, encouraging and directing her as they explored all the different items on the huge platter he'd ordered for them to share.

Ellie picked up a piece of each and put them on her plate. "Speaking of things that go together, did *you* know Mick and Marny are a thing?"

Nash laughed.

"What?"

He shook his head, still chuckling. "The way you say *thing*."

She gave him a mock scowl, unable to be truly mean because of the way his eyes sparkled when he laughed. "Are you making fun of my accent?"

"No, no," he said, reaching for his water glass. "Well, okay, maybe a little. There are just some words that… well, they sound so *Texan*."

"Oh, and that's such a source of laughs given that we are, in fact, in the Texas state capital."

"I shouldn't tease, I know."

Ellie pointed at him with the end of her chopsticks. "No, you should not. Besides, I have two brothers. I have a black belt in teasing, so you'd lose."

"Okay, yes, I did know Mick and Marny are—" he gave the word a very neutral pronunciation "—a thing. Mick told me the other day."

"And yet you still put them together when we cleaned the bison brushes." She gave him a look. "You're a softie."

"You can't tell me you don't have a soft spot for Marny. I've seen the way you work with her. She was all attitude and apathy that first week, but I feel like she's coming around."

Marny had been the hardest sell of all the girls, but Ellie dug her stubborn Buckton heels in and kept trying to connect with the girl. She was making progress— just not nearly as much as she'd hoped. "She's still got a monster chip on her shoulder. At first, I was pretty sure she had something against me—though I had no idea what. So I just did what Gran told me."

"What was that?"

"I loved on her harder. Gran says the only way to fight hate is with love. I may not be there when it comes to Derek, but I have really tried to meet Marny's every dark look or snide remark with nothing but faith and love." She selected another piece of sushi and rolled her eyes. "But I tell you, it's been hard. She's tested me. She's tested my faith. But I just kept pushing closer, asking questions, paying attention."

Nash looked at her with admiration. There was something else in his eyes, too, but she chose to pretend she did not see it. "Then she finally talked about her home life, and my heart broke open. It sounds terrible, Nash. She's practically ignored. Here I've got more family attention than I could ever want, and she tells me stories about her dad staying out drinking all night and then coming home mean and demanding she make him breakfast before she leaves for school."

"It's not hard to see why they connect with each other. Mick's story doesn't sound much better." Nash dug into his bowl of rice. "They get to you after a while. You tell yourself not to get all caught up in their lives, but you do."

And then they turn around and shoot you. He didn't say it, but the sentiment was there, broadcast in the pain and regret that tightened his features. *Hearts can be broken in more than one way*, she thought as she allowed herself a long gaze into his eyes. "Do you think it will work?" she asked, because someone needed to say something to break the all-too-potent silence.

"Will what work?"

"Theo's program. Do you think it will turn some of these kids around like he wants? I mean, you've been involved in programs like this before. You ought to know."

"It really depends on the kids. We give them a little grace and compassion, show them we believe in them, but it's up to them what they do with that belief. Some accept it and build on it. Others hold on to it for a second and then throw it away. And some never stop pushing it away." He sat back in his chair. "It's a lot like the parable of the sower and the seeds, when you think about it. Most of it depends on the kind of soil the seed gets and what kind of weeds are there ready to choke it out. Thing is, not too much of that is in our control."

"No wonder I've been praying so hard. It's like these girls never leave my mind. Everything they say sticks with me, and the little hurts just nag at me. I'll be a wreck as a mother if this is any indication."

"Did you and Derek plan to have kids?"

Now, there was a volatile subject. "We talked about

it. We both wanted them, but there was a bit of friction about when. Derek wanted to wait until he opened his own restaurant."

"That sounds like smart thinking," Nash offered.

"Sure, until you realize that goal was years away. Not that Derek wasn't gaining notoriety fast enough to up the timetable, but that still would have put us starting a family a long time from now."

"And you want to start sooner than that?"

Ellie slumped against the booth. "You know, before Wylene's I would have said yes. But seeing all my high school friends as moms, their lives all taken up with family stuff, well, I'm not so sure anymore. It seems like such a huge responsibility to carry all that off. I'm a bit scared of it, to tell the truth."

"That's because you're spooked right now. And based on what you've told me, it doesn't sound like Derek would have been much of an equal partner in the parenting department. I see it in you, Ellie. With the right guy at your side, you'll be a spectacular mom." When Ellie and he both sensed the weight of that statement press down a bit too heavy between them, he added, "I hope he comes along soon."

"Yeah," she agreed, her heart a tumbling ball of confusion. "Me, too."

Chapter Fourteen

At the next program session the following afternoon, Ellie looked around the room. Her heart glowed to hear the splendid sound of needles clicking. Five of the six girls had caught on in a jiffy, and while Ina Jean was struggling a bit, the girl's face was scrunched with determination to master the stitches.

"See," Ellie said, pointing to the row Ina Jean had just finished. "Not a single mistake in that one. You're catching on fast."

"Look at my rows." Dianne—always quick to lead but just as quick to boast—held up a nearly finished cotton piece.

Ellie had given each of the girls brightly colored cotton yarn to make a dishcloth—a fast project with a yarn that made it easy to see the stitches. Ellie saw Ina Jean's face fall in defeat. Her progress, far behind that of the other girls, threatened to steal her confidence.

"You are fast, Dianne. I'll give you that. But take a look at your rows. If you slow down a bit, your stitches will be more even. This isn't a race." Ellie directed her attention to the girl steadily stitching beside Dianne. "It's much more about the process, at least for me. Does anyone know where Marny is?"

"I saw her at school," Caroline said. "She didn't say anything about not coming today."

"Well, maybe something came up at the last minute," Ellie replied, trying not to read anything into the girl's absence. "Tell me, Caroline, do you like the feel of this yarn?"

Caroline, who had the most artistic bent in the group, held up her lavender-colored cotton and ran it between her fingers. "It's okay. I mean for a dishcloth and all. I'd want something softer for a scarf or whatever."

Ellie had been waiting for just such a comment. "Then take a feel of this." She pulled a hank of bison-silk blend—exactly the kind she'd envisioned for Blue Thorn Fibers—from her bag and handed it to Caroline.

"Wow." Caroline's face registered her appreciation of the exquisite feel Ellie knew well. "I'd wear anything made from this."

"Exactly my point." Ellie caught the eye of each girl in the room. "Some low-cost fibers are good for some things—basic, sturdy things like dishcloths and socks— and others are worth the expense for things that go next to your skin."

"Socks go next to your skin," Lucy said, stretching out those long legs of hers as Caroline handed her the bison-silk yarn. "I despise lumpy socks. My mom buys awful ones from the resale store and says 'They're just socks.' But I hate the way they feel."

Ellie remembered high school and what it had felt like to wear something she hadn't liked or that felt woefully out of fashion. During the harder years at Blue Thorn, she'd mostly worn resale shop clothes that had made her feel frumpy. Her brain pulled up an image of willowy Lucy with a diaphanous lacework shawl draped over her shoulders—that girl would look and feel like a princess. "You're right, Lucy. Some things like socks ought to be both—they need to be basic and sturdy, but you want them to feel soft and wonderful. In fact, I'm with you one hundred percent on the socks. And that's the great thing about bison fiber—it's really strong and really soft at the same time."

"And probably really expensive." Lucy had such resignation in her voice as she handed the hank over to the next girl.

"Crazy expensive," Marny called from the doorway. "I looked it up on the internet at school. Who can afford seventy dollars for something stupid like yarn?" She didn't come in the room, only stood in the doorway.

Ellie didn't know what to make of a statement like that. It was clear from Marny's eyes and the jut of the arm on her hip, however, that she was not in a good mood.

"It's steep. I'll grant you that," Ellie agreed as she tried to catch Marny's eye. "But remember socks made with bison yarn can be twice as warm and wear twice as long as ones made with wool. That makes it a good investment. Which is why I'm investing two hanks in each of you girls, so you'll have something really wonderful by the end of our time together. After all, you helped us gather the hair and down. You've earned it. So you all will be the first to receive hanks of Blue Thorn bison yarn."

"What am I gonna do with $150 worth of yarn?" Marny scoffed. "I could buy a ton of new clothes with that much money."

The other girls seemed happy at the gift, their eyes popping at Ellie's gesture. "Really?" said one. "You'd do that?" balked another. With a chill Ellie realized these girls may have never received a gift as indulgent as the hanks of expensive yarn. Marny's remark just went to show Ellie how their lives were clearly about frugal necessities—luxurious treats happened rarely, if ever.

Every woman—especially every young woman— ought to feel cherished enough to be given lovely things, even if it's just every once in a while. The past few weeks had showed her that in no uncertain terms. The urge to run out and buy each of them something perfect, exquisite and absolutely frivolous welled up so strongly within Ellie it was a good thing they couldn't all fit in her car. Here she was feeling boxed in by what Derek had done to her, and this moment showed all the freedoms she enjoyed. She was her own person, making her own money, pursuing a career in a satisfying field. When she was ready, she could work anywhere in the country—in the world, for that matter.

"I don't need yarn like that. I can't stay in this thing anyway. I just came to tell you I won't be coming back."

"Marny, no." Ellie stood up. "You're the best knitter in here. I don't want you to leave us."

"I don't have time for silly crafts. I need to go get me

a job, not sit here and play with yarn." With no more than that, Marny turned and walked down the hallway.

Should she go after the girl? Let her go and try to connect later when things weren't so tense? Ellie looked around the room for clues about what to do.

"I don't think it's silly," Caroline said quietly. "I like being here." Looking into Caroline's eyes, seeing the commitment there and the pride in the knitting she'd completed, healed some of the hurt Ellie had felt at Marny's harsh words.

No, it did more than that. The paralysis of her broken engagement finally began to fall away for Ellie. These girls had so little affirmation. They were so desperate for someone to believe in them. Ellie had known life wasn't over when Derek had cheated on her, but today was the first time it really felt as though life was moving on, and she was happy with the direction it was going. Happy that she'd been brought home, where she could build a connection with these girls and maybe make a difference in their lives.

It wasn't actually going to cost her one hundred and fifty dollars per girl to give them the yarn. She was simply giving them the first spun hanks from the fiber Blue Thorn had. They didn't have enough raw fiber to make twelve pure bison hanks, so Ellie had arranged to use her own money to make the hanks a bison-silk blend. Seeing what she just saw, Ellie would gladly pay double whatever it cost. It felt like the smallest of prices for what these girls were giving her—perspective.

"No, it's not," Ellie declared. "I believe in each of you as knitters. As young women. You deserve to have amazing things in your lives, and I want you to have the nicest yarn around to launch your knitting hobby. And I can't wait to see all the wonderful things—" she made sure to catch Caroline's eye "—I know you're going to make with it."

Nash poked his head into the girls' classroom. "Break time."

It had only taken one session for Nash and Ellie to discover the kids were hungry after school. Snacks— provided by Grannie Buckton, who'd evidently jumped at the chance when Ellie mentioned a need—had become a welcome midprogram break. In addition to gobbling down goodies, break time also gave him and Ellie a chance to check in with each other's progress and problem solve anything that had come up.

Today something had definitely come up. "Everything okay?" he asked as soon as they had a moment together.

"Not at all." Ellie relayed Marny's angry exit and her cutting remarks. He could see how deeply the jab had affected Ellie. He'd known something like this would happen sooner or later. "You're the teen expert," she pleaded. "What do I do?"

He wasn't an expert, but he had enough experience to expect a blowup from someone at some point. The fact that it was Marny didn't surprise him—Ellie considered the girl her most difficult student. "I'm not sure you can do anything. At least right now. I'll see what I can get out of Mick, but probably the best thing is to just let it sit for a day and then go try to find out what was at the heart of that explosion."

Ellie pulled on a lock of her hair. "I hate to see her leave, Nash. She needs this, even if she won't admit it."

Nash put a hand on her elbow. "Well, maybe now's the time to issue the challenge. We might be able to coax her back on the premise of needing even teams."

They'd discussed the idea of a mutual challenge for the final session where the girls taught the guys a domestic skill like sewing on a button and the guys taught the girls a basic automotive skill like how to change a tire.

"Well, we can't move it up to next week. They're scheduled to clean the brushes at the ranch then." She frowned. "It's going to be such a great visit, I can't bear for Marny to miss it. Gunner wants to give the kids our blue bandannas when they come back. All the family and employees of Blue Thorn carry them. It'll mark their official installment as members of the Blue Thorn team, and he's going to let them come back all the way through shedding season."

"That's great," Nash agreed. It meant the program would continue to have effects that would last far beyond the weeks they met. "We definitely don't want Marny to miss that."

"It's one of those great 'everybody wins' situations, Nash. The work gets done, the kids get new experiences and get to know the ranch, and they seem to have fun."

"I agree. It's a clear success." He put a hand on her arm. "Look, try not to let this bump in the road with Marny get to you. The fact that she's pushing back just means that you're getting through to her. It means you're making a difference." He stared at Ellie for a longer moment than he should have, sensing her commitment, feeling her hurt.

"Miss Ellie," Dianne shouted from across the room. "Tell Davey to stop making jokes about knitting only being for grannies in rocking chairs." Dianne turned to Davey and pursed her lips. "I saw a website yesterday with a picture of guys knitting ski hats, and they were a lot cooler and cuter than you."

"The hats maybe," Davey teased. "But not the guys. They don't come cuter and cooler than me." Nash set down his coffee, ready to step in.

"I know dogs that are cuter and cooler than you," Dianne shot back.

"Maybe puppies in Alaska. Where they need ski hats. We sure don't need 'em here."

"I'd never turn down anything you made for me," Leon cooed theatrically to Dianne. A chorus of oohs and aaws set everyone to laughing.

Nash walked to the center of the room. "I'd expect any of you gentlemen to kindly accept anything someone handmade for you. Just as I'd expect any of you ladies to graciously thank the man who changed your tire by the side of the road."

"I would," Ina Jean said, tugging on one braid. "If they did it right." More laughter.

"Just food for thought, y'all," Ellie cut in. "But I am of the belief that a man can knit just fine if he likes, and a woman can change a tire if she's of a mind to. Am I right, Mr. Nash?"

"You heard Miss Ellie," Nash said. "And we're going to see just how well that theory holds up in two weeks.

A contest of skills, guys against girls. So don't you be making yarn jokes, boys, or it may come back to haunt you. And you ladies might end up getting a little grease under your fingernails before we're done here."

"But we'll be short without Marny," Ina Jean complained.

"What do you mean without Marny?" Mick asked. Clearly, Marny hadn't yet shared her plans to quit the class with him. Nash wondered just what that meant.

"She left us," Lucy said sharply. "Came in today just to make fun of us and tell us she's not coming back."

"She can't not come back," Mick contested.

"Well, you'd better tell that to your girlfriend," Lucy replied. "'Cause from what I saw, she is out of here."

Mick rose to leave, but Nash put his hand on the boy's shoulder. "Hang on there. You can talk to Marny after class, but it didn't sound like she wanted company at the moment." He turned to the whole group. "But we all want Marny back, and I hope you'll do your best to convince her of that before next week." He looked at his watch. "Okay, break's over. Back to your programs." He caught Ellie's eye. "Let's figure out how to handle this when we have our meeting with Theo tomorrow."

Chapter Fifteen

Ellie's cell phone rang Thursday morning. "Ellie, I know Nash said we were meeting at eleven, but can you come over now?" asked Pastor Theo. "Things have taken a bit of a bad turn here, and I think you could help."

Ellie had on farm work clothes and hadn't yet dressed for going into town. "Sure. What's going on?"

"I'd rather not go into it on the phone. Just get here as quickly as you can. Actually, no—don't come here first. Go to Nash's house. I expect he's home. I checked with Don and he's not at the sheriff's office. Bring him here when he's ready—but I'm warning you, that may take a while."

"Why? What on earth happened?"

"I really can't go into it here, but the ballistics test from your bison evidently came back with disturbing results. I want the three of us to talk about what to do from here, but from his phone call to me, Nash isn't in a mood to have a rational discussion. I know I probably should send Don over, but God brought you to mind, so I'm trusting that."

Ellie pulled a nicer shirt out of her closet and began looking for her sandals. "Sure. I'll go to his house. And if he's not there, I'll call you and we'll find him."

Who could those tests have implicated that would make Nash so upset? There was only one way to find out.

"Gran," Ellie called as she came downstairs brushing her hair. "I've got to go out. Tell Gunner to call my cell if he needs me." She wasn't ready to tell Gunner and Gran that Nash likely knew who the shooter was. She couldn't be certain yet, and that was probably best done by official police procedures anyway. She knew Gunner—he'd press charges as hard as he could, whoever it was.

She didn't have to ring the doorbell to know Nash wasn't in the house—the sound coming from the garage let her know where to find him. The loud clang of hammer on steel rang through the air as she walked up the drive to his open garage door. Nash had his back to her, stripped to a sweat-soaked white T-shirt that clung to his skin. He was hurling a sledgehammer at a mangled piece of steel. She stayed back, warned to keep her distance by the sheer ferocity of his swings.

After half a minute, he exhaled loudly, chest heaving from the exertion, and rested the sledgehammer on the ground. She took one step into the garage.

"Nash?"

He turned, and the look on his face practically made her take a step back. Sharp features framed hard, cold eyes. His whole body looked as if it was at war—strung tight and ready for battle. At the same time, a bone-weary exhaustion lurked under all the tension. He looked like a man who had fought for a long time and was ready to give up. "Theo?"

He let the sledgehammer fall against the nearby workbench, which made Ellie feel safe enough to come closer. "He called me, yes. He didn't tell me what happened, but I'm pretty sure I know." She held his gaze, sensing the frustration that radiated off him like heat off a stove. "Who?"

"Mick."

Mick? Her wildest guess would have never been Mick. He was the closest to Nash, looked up to him as the mentor figure Mick's own father clearly wasn't. If she'd had to choose which boy was getting the most out of the program, it would have been Mick, without a doubt. The punch in her gut must have been pale in comparison to what Nash was feeling. "It couldn't be Mick." That felt foolish to say, but it seemed so impossible that Mick would be shooting Blue Thorn bison. "It *can't* be Mick."

Nash took off his safety glasses, which just made the ice in his eyes that much sharper. "Well, there's a small chance it could be Mick's father—the rifle's registered to him—but I don't think there's any point in fooling ourselves."

"I'm sorry." Really, what was there to say to this?

Her apology tightened his already tense features. "*You're* sorry? This kid takes my time, your time, helps out on your ranch, gets to know the both of us and then shoots your animals. And you're sorry? I'm not sorry. I'm furious. I've been taking it out on this hunk of metal because, believe me, if I even see that punk right now I don't know what I'd do to him." He flung the work gloves off his hands. "To put you and your family in danger like that. To kill one of your animals. The stupidity. The sheer cruelty of it." He looked at her. "And don't forget this started before the program. The casing I found earlier, from my first visits here? It matches. He came in and took what we had to offer even after trying to hurt your family. What kind of human being does that?"

"I don't know. I can't make sense of this." It was bad enough when some unnamed person was taking shots at the ranch, but to learn it was someone she knew, someone she'd helped… The betrayal of this piled up on the betrayal of Derek and Katie, and suddenly it felt as if the whole world was ganging up to do her in. "What do we do?" Tears threatened all too quickly— she couldn't go to pieces now, not with Nash looking like a bomb ready to go off.

"I don't know," Nash growled, kicking an empty soda can by his feet. "I know what I ought to do, but I'm far too angry to do it."

"Maybe you should let Don handle it."

That jolted his head upright. "I will *not* let Don handle this. I want this kid to stare me in the face when I charge him with killing your animal. Endangering your family. And you. I want Mick to feel the full weight of what he's done."

Ellie had little doubt about that. Nash looked as if

he was ready to come down on Mick like his worst nightmare. Was that good or bad? Mick had done something stupid and dangerous, but he was still only seventeen—he couldn't even be charged as an adult, from what she guessed.

Theo walked into the garage behind her. "So, we have a problem on our hands."

"I'll say," said Ellie. She was hurt and angry, but Nash looked downright explosive.

"I decided just to come over here and not wait. It's probably better to have this conversation out of my office anyway. So, how are we going to handle this?" Theo asked as he leaned against a sawhorse, motioning for Ellie and Nash to take the stools in front of the workbench.

"It's pretty clear what has to happen," Nash said as he sat down. "We take Mick in, get his fingerprints, match them to the rifle and charge him—and maybe also his father—with the crime."

Theo folded his hands. "I think there's more to it than that. Mick is a member of our church, a young man we've been helping. We need some wisdom and grace as well as the justice you seek."

"I have no grace for that kid," Nash ground out.

"Look, I'm hurt by what he's done," Ellie began. "And I'm confused as to why on earth he'd do it, but I can see Theo's point. We've got to think about this. The other kids—the whole church, probably the whole town—will be watching how we handle this."

Theo turned to her. "Will Gunner want to press charges?"

"Absolutely. He's angry, and he has a right to be. This has messed everyone up at the worst possible time. The family is frightened, the bison are stressed, which makes them volatile—and they're already tough to handle in calving season. And that's before factoring in the monetary loss of the animal he shot. It's hit Gunner hard. The man has a baby of his own on the way."

"All things Mick knows and chose to ignore," Nash said. "We ought to make an example of him."

"Are you sure that's the way to go here, Nash?" Theo looked concerned. Even Ellie had been startled by the severity of Nash's words. This was a side of Nash she'd always known must be there—the warrior, the enforcer—but hadn't really seen before. "Even you have to realize you're not entirely objective on this."

"We've invested so much into Mick and the other kids," Ellie said. "I can't understand why he'd do this. It so…senseless."

Nash put back on his shirt. "I'm bringing him in. The only question is do I pull him out of school in front of everyone or wait until after?"

Ellie had a vision of Nash walking Mick out of school in handcuffs. Was that really necessary? Would that straighten out a kid like Mick or just send him farther down the wrong path? She knew which Gunner would choose—and a part of her was as angry as her brother. A smaller part of her was shouting, *Wait, stop! There's another way!*

"Don't you have to talk to Gunner first? Official procedure or something?"

"I have enough evidence to bring him in for questioning now. All I need is his father's consent, and believe me, I'll get it." Nash looked at Ellie. "I've gotten enough out of my system that I'll be calm about it, but I want to be the one to do it. I'll go pick up his dad and be waiting for him at lunch hour. After I've questioned him, I'll talk to Gunner and we *will* arrest him."

Theo turned to Ellie. "Let's see if we can get the rest of the kids gathered at church after school. I can talk to them, help them understand what's happened and why."

That seemed like a good plan. Still, it all swirled around her head. "Mick, shooting at the Blue Thorn? I just can't believe it. Why?"

"We'll know in a few hours."

Mick sat fidgeting in the guest chair of Nash's desk in the sheriff's office, rocking it back and forth on its casters and jiggling one knee up and down. The boy was alone. When Nash talked to Mick's father, the man openly admitted giving Mick access to the now-missing rifle. He seemed more worried about the weapon than his son, surprising Nash by waiving his right to be present for Mick's questioning. What kind of father treated his own son that way?

Don stood in the corner behind Mick and looked on. He had only barely consented to let Nash take the lead in interrogating Mick. No one was operating under the delusion Nash could be objective about this, but Nash had convinced Don that letting Mick see the full force of Nash's anger might be useful. These kids were sorely lacking in a sense of consequences, so better an angry deputy than another dead animal.

Nash started with simple facts. "A bison was found killed on the Blue Thorn Ranch Sunday morning. We know it was shot by your father's rifle."

"So?" Mick barked back, defensive and afraid.

"Your dad says you have use of that rifle. He also says he doesn't know where it is right now. He told us you do."

Mick shrugged. "Father of the year, my dad, huh?"

Nash took a breath. In fact, they'd found the rifle stashed in a garbage can behind Mick's home. Kids were never very creative in hiding weapons; they were always sure they'd never get caught. Nash sat right across from Mick, letting the frayed edges of his temper show. "I'm going to make this very simple. One question. Did you shoot the bison?

"I didn't shoot that big buffalo. It wasn't me."

Nash sat back. "Who said the bison was big? How do you know it wasn't a calf that got shot?"

"Well." Mick backpedaled. "I just figured no one would be mean enough to shoot a baby one." He looked everywhere but at Nash, clearly aware of the hole he was digging for himself.

Nash leaned toward Mick again, anger and sympathy warring in his chest. Mick was a clever, determined kid, but his dad had pretty much hung him out to dry. Mick could do so much more with his life than throw it away down this current path. Here was a kid looking for the deepest hurt possible—one that was also a cry for help. Nash made the effort to keep his voice even. "This will go much better for everyone, Mick, if you just level with me. You're still seventeen, which means we have some leeway here, but not if you don't cooperate." He stared at Mick until the boy finally met his eyes. "The person who shot the bison will go to jail."

"You mean like *murder*?" Mick's fingers began drumming against the chair arms. The consequences of his actions were finally sinking in.

"Technically, it's criminal mischief, but believe me, that's serious enough to get you into a heap of trouble. The Bucktons will likely press full charges. And they should. No one here believes this was an accidental shooting. No one."

Mick shook his head. Nash's instincts told him the boy was about to break. He swallowed the urge to take the kid by his shoulders and shake some sense into him, but that wouldn't help anyone. Everything would go easier—not easy, but easier—if Mick would just own up to what he'd done.

When no reply came, Nash unclenched his own fists, coming around to lean against the desk and deliberately using his height to tower over Mick. "I'll ask you again. Did you shoot the bison at Blue Thorn Ranch?"

Mick squirmed in his chair. "No. I tell you, it wasn't me."

Nash's frustration got the better of him, and he pushed off the table to pace the office. Don was right— he had totally lost the ability to keep calm about this.

"I didn't do it," Mick repeated, his voice pitching higher.

The fax machine in the corner of the office began to buzz and churn out paper. They were expecting the lab's report on fingerprints found on the rifle. In a matter of seconds, Mick's guilt would be sealed.

Nash nodded toward the machine. "We already have the rifle, Mick. That's probably the lab report right now. If that paper says those are your prints on that rifle, you'd best start talking." Nash nodded to Don, who walked to the machine and stood over it.

"It's from my house—of course my prints are gonna be on it." Mick was grasping at straws, his nerves beyond tight.

"Tell me now, Mick. I won't be able to help you otherwise."

"I didn't shoot the gun!" Mick yelped.

Nash lost his temper. "You're lying!" he shouted at Mick.

"Maybe not" came Don's voice from over the fax machine.

Both Nash and Mick turned to look at Don, who was holding up the sheet of paper.

"Oh, man," Mick moaned, his hand wiping the back of his neck.

"There's a third set of prints on the gun. And the ones on the trigger aren't Mick's."

"Oh, man. Oh, man," Mick kept saying, rocking a little.

Nash felt eleven things at once. Regret at his certainty that Mick had betrayed him, uncertainty as to what it meant that Mick hadn't done the shooting, worry over who had and several other emotions. He kept his mouth shut, unsure what to say.

"Which means, son—" Don kept his voice very low

as he walked over and stood in front of Mick "—that while you may not have shot that animal, you know who did. Accessory to a crime is still a crime. Don't you think for one moment that you are not still in a heap of trouble. The best thing you can do now is tell us the truth."

"Who did it, Mick?" Nash practically ground the words out through clenched teeth. This surely meant that more than one of his students had betrayed his trust—just when he thought the burn couldn't go any deeper. "I know you know, and believe me, I am losing patience here."

Mick bit his lip and clutched the chair arms.

"Who shot the bison, Mick?" Nash asked more loudly.

"Don't be stupid, son," Don said over Mick's shoulder. "Tell us what you know."

"Who shot the bison?" Nash yelled louder than he ought to have.

"Marny!" Mick blurted out, his face going nearly red with the stress of the admission. "It was Marny, okay? She did it."

Mick curled in on himself as Nash felt a wave of shock shoot through his limbs. Marny? How? Why?

"Marny Fuller shot that animal?" Don asked. "With your father's rifle?"

"Marny?" Nash repeated, still stunned. Of all the admissions he'd expected, this was not one of them.

"Yeah, Marny. Now you know why I didn't want to say, okay?"

"Son, this is a long way from okay. You've got some explaining to do."

Mick's face went from flushed to pale, looking as though he might be sick. Nash, still struggling to put the pieces together, grabbed another chair and pulled it up next to the boy. "Tell me what happened." Half of him was relieved that his faith in the boy hadn't been misplaced entirely, while the other half was shocked at Marny's nearly equal betrayal.

"Our dads hate Miss Ellie's family."

Nash couldn't quite see how that fit in, but he urged Mick to continue. "Go on."

"Mostly Marny's dad, but he and my dad talk a lot since they're both out of work. They spend a lot of time down at Lonesome's, you know?"

Lonesome's was the bar just down the block from Shorty's Pizza. Nash or Don got at least one call a week to break up a fight or some such nonsense at the roadhouse. Not exactly an uplifting place to spend a lot of time.

"What do your dads have against the Bucktons?" Nash couldn't see how any grievance warranted what was going on.

"Marny's dad worked a day or two at the Blue Thorn a while back, and he thought it'd be permanent, I guess. Only it wasn't. Marny's dad drinks a lot." In a heartbreaking show of misplaced loyalty, Mick looked up at Don. "I mean, he's never hit her or anything like that, but Dad says he's a mean drunk, and I've seen it. He yells, mostly. Sometimes at her, but mostly at anybody he thinks ought to have hired him."

Nash still wasn't seeing a strong enough connection. If Marny's dad had only worked a day or two on the ranch, that might explain why he hadn't shown up on the employees list. "So Jerry Fuller thinks he should be working at the Blue Thorn?"

"No, nothing like that. He holds a grudge, and I don't think he'd work there now even if they asked him. But he—well, he and my dad, actually—were both ready to get jobs building those fancy houses that were gonna go up last year. Those were supposed to be good-paying jobs, Dad said. Marny's dad said things were gonna be looking up for him and her. She wouldn't have to go to Waco to live with her mama or anything like that."

Don came around and sat on Nash's desk. "You mean Ramble Acres? The DelTex condo development that got nixed last spring?"

"That's the one. My dad said even I could probably get a better job working on that site than working at Shorty's all summer. I could probably even buy a new car."

Now it was starting to make sense. Nash had been told that the Buckton family had been the target of some nasty dealing by DelTex in order to gain the water access needed to build Ramble Acres. To keep from having the land rights forced away from them, the Bucktons had exposed the company's underhanded practices. As a result, the Ramble Acres project had died and taken a lot of potential jobs with it. It wasn't hard to see how these two kids had decided the Bucktons had hurt them. "So your dads think the Bucktons took their jobs away. And your lives are worse on account of it."

Mick picked at a rip in his jeans. "If Marny's dad sends her to Waco, I don't know what I'll do. I'll never see her again." He looked up at Nash. "Marny's dad ain't no picnic, but her mama's worse, if you ask me. Marny'd say the same."

"So you decided to get back at the Bucktons for what they'd done to you." It still made no sense given how much time Marny had spent with Ellie, but who could say how a teenage brain put facts together? *Oh, Ellie.* She was going to be stung by this. Badly. At a time when she was already hurting. She'd poured as much time and attention into Marny as Nash had into Mick. Now Marny's outburst at the church program made a sick sort of sense. *What a mess of pain this is, Lord. How on earth do we find our way out of it?*

Nash's gut sank lower when he remembered something. "The first shooting took place even before we met. Did you and Marny do that one?"

"We were just messing around then. Marny is a really good shot. I thought at first she was just letting off steam or something—she thought it was fun to scare the herd. I didn't think we'd actually hurt anyone."

If Nash had a dime for every time he'd heard that phrase… "But you did. Do you get how serious this is, Mick? I know you were trying to protect Marny, but do you hear what I'm saying?"

Mick looked at Nash. "I get it. I get it."

"Do you?" Don stood up from the desk.

"What happens now?" Mick practically whined. Nash fought the twin urges to hug and shake the boy.

Things could go any number of directions now—most of them bad.

"Now we bring in your dad, Marny and her dad. Things are going to get very messy from here."

Mick's face sank as he realized just how far this tangle spread. The boy put his head in his hands and cursed, and Nash couldn't blame him.

"Take his statement," Don said. "And I'll find Miss Fuller. Then we'll ride out to the Bucktons' and let them know what's up."

"Let me talk to Ellie before you talk to Gunner, okay? This is going to hit her hard, and she deserves a heads-up before we hit the whole family with this."

Don paused a bit before nodding. "Well, I suppose another hour won't pretty this up none. Mick, give me Marny's cell number, 'cause I know you've got it."

While Mick replied, Nash pulled out the statement form, and the whole world started its downward spiral from there.

Chapter Sixteen

It had been a long time since Nash had been that surprised. Marny was the one who'd shot the bison? He'd held his anger in check while he'd questioned Mick, but hadn't been prepared for what he'd learned. Now he had to tell Ellie, had to watch her investment in the girl go up in flames the way he'd just experienced. The cruelty of it—the sheer unfairness of heaping so much pain and betrayal on one woman at one time—gnawed at his gut and made his fingers anxiously flex and fist as he walked into the church.

"They're in here," Dottie Howe said as she pointed to one of the Sunday School classrooms, where Theo and Ellie were talking with all of the after-school kids. Well, nearly all. Mick was still at the station and no one could find Marny. Now Nash knew why.

"Is it true?" Dottie asked, her voice a cringe. She clearly knew what had happened—probably half of Martins Gap had heard that Mick had been brought in on suspicion of shooting the Blue Thorn bison. Right now only Don and Nash knew that wasn't the whole story.

"Best not to say anything at this point, Dottie. I'll keep Theo informed as things progress, though, I promise you."

Nash peered in the window of the classroom door and knocked. The whole room startled at his face in the glass. When he entered in full uniform, the air thickened. "Miss Ellie, may I see you for a moment?"

Ellie smoothed her palms against her pant legs. "Sure."

"Is Mick going to jail?" Lucy asked, clearly upset. Nash was glad to see most of the kids were rattled by what they'd heard. That was a much better response than apathy or, worse yet, admiration.

"It's a bit early to say anything like that." It was a stall, but it was also a half-truth. Based on what he'd just learned, Nash quite honestly wasn't sure what the next move ought to be.

Ellie stepped out of the classroom and shut the door behind her. "What's happened?"

He pulled her into the next room and closed the door. "Well, I brought Mick in for questioning. Alone. His dad waived his right to be present, fine and dandy with leaving his son to twist in the wind. I'd like to have a word or two with that guy."

Ellie ran an agitated hand through her hair. "To be so…disregarded like that. I can't imagine how that hurts someone Mick's age."

You'll find out more about what that's like in a minute, warned a voice in Nash's head. Ellie had told him she lost her mom at thirteen and her dad when she was just out of business school, but she still knew nothing but love and support from her family. That was half of why Derek's unfaithfulness had hit her so hard. She trusted the people who loved her to have her back, and up until recently, they had. He hated to be the one to pry another crack of betrayal into the safe wall that had been around her life.

She caught his expression. "There's something else, isn't there?" She threw her glance to the ceiling. "What could make this worse?"

Nash moved to the windowsill and leaned against it. "While we were talking to him, the evidence report on the rifle came in. We needed to run prints on the weapon in addition to ballistics. The rifle is registered to Mick's father, and Mick's prints were definitely on it."

Ellie had caught his expression. "Well, that can't have been much of a surprise."

There wasn't really an easy way to say it, so Nash chose direct fact. "But so were Marny's. Ellie, Marny is the one who shot at the bison. Mick came clean once he knew we had a third set of fingerprints. Mick gave her the rifle, but the shooter is… Ellie, it's Marny."

He watched the same disbelief he'd known wash across Ellie's features as she slumped against the wall next to him. "Marny? Marny's been shooting at my bison?"

Her voice broke a bit on the word *my.* The pain washed over her face the way it had crept over his own heart—it was the worst kind of betrayal to think someone you'd invested in, someone you cared for and had tried to see the good in, could turn around and do you harm. If life offered emotional sucker punches, this was one of its most lethal.

And hadn't she just had the only thing that hurt worse from Derek? To have care and charity thrown back in your face was one thing, but to have your love and loyalty stomped on—and with your best friend? Nash felt the news he delivered turn his gut as if he'd eaten something toxic.

"Why?" The word was almost a moan, a knife blade to Nash's heart.

"Mick gave me some idea, but I won't really know until I can bring her in. It has something to do with her father."

"Her father? How? What grudge could he have against Blue Thorn?"

In the weeks since Nash had met her, Ellie had become possessive—protective, even—of the ranch. At first she'd called it "the ranch," but now she often said "our ranch" or even "my ranch." Some part of him rejoiced at her reconnection with her family land— mostly because a growing part of his heart was wishing she would stay. The dangerous truth was that he was falling for her, and at the worst possible time.

"According to Mick, Jerry felt the Ramble Acres development would change things for him and the whole town. When your family shut that DelTex project down, it seems he blamed the Bucktons for taking away his chance at work."

Ellie pushed off the wall, hugging herself in a

protective way that made Nash's throat tighten. "That's ridiculous."

Of course it was. Nothing about this made any logical sense whatsoever.

"We did nothing to hurt Marny's family," Ellie continued as she walked along the bank of windows that looked out on the church's little garden. "What DelTex was trying to do with Ramble Acres was wrong. Gunner and Brooke and Gran did the right thing. And even if some people would have benefitted from Ramble Acres, nothing warrants shooting innocent animals." She looked up at Nash. "I can't picture it. I know Marny's no sweet, innocent little girl, but I still can't pull up an image of her sighting a rifle at our animals." She looked at Nash with alarm in her eyes. "What's next? Sighting a rifle at us? We invited her—her and Mick—onto our land. We put our faith in them."

"Near as I can tell, she's been fed a daily dose of bitterness and anger by her father. He talked about hurting the herd as payback. The reason she wasn't at the program last time was because Jerry found out about your involvement and the group's visits to the ranch. I think you were getting through to her at the same time her dad was telling her you were the root of everything bad happening to her. Confusion messed with her mind. She couldn't figure out how to care and hate for the same thing at the same time, and choosing your care meant rejecting her father."

"She ought to reject him," Ellie snapped, her anger rising.

"You said yourself Gunner rejected your father. You

saw how it messed him up for a while." Ellie had given him a short version of Gunner's sketchy past, how he'd done a lot of regrettable things before making peace with the family. "What girl wouldn't snap under the emotional strain Marny knows? I'm not saying what she did was right or even forgivable. But I can connect the dots and see how it happened. She convinced Mick to take his father's rifle. I don't think she was consciously firing at you or your animals. She was firing at everything wrong in her life."

"I helped her," Ellie blurted out in a voice tight with pain. "I gave her money so she could buy a new hair dryer. I prayed for her. And all this time…"

Nash couldn't stop himself from taking a few steps toward her. He knew what this felt like. He knew the jagged edge of this realization and how deeply it cut. Hadn't he pounded a car panel with a sledgehammer to work it out of his own system? It was bad enough to swallow it himself, but to watch Ellie buckle under it tore him to pieces. He put a hand on her shoulder. "Ellie…"

She shrugged him off. "Does everyone think I'm a doormat they can walk over? Do I have a Hurt Me sign on my back?"

He didn't have an answer—for either himself or for her.

"Why does this kind of stuff keep happening to me? Am I some kind of magnet for people who think it's perfectly fine to hurt me?"

"No," he said, catching her hand as it flailed in the air. "You care. Deeply. And you expect others to care as deeply as you do. Up until now, the people who you care about have always been on your side. That's a blessing a lot of people have never had. Now you've been hit from all sides with people who threw that care back in your face." He gripped her hand more tightly "I hate that it's happened to you. Over and over like this. There's nothing, *nothing* wrong in how you care. It's who you are."

"Yeah?" She pulled her arm from his grasp. "Well, *who I am* feels like a great big punching bag right now. You know, I thought you were overreacting a bit back there in the garage, but if I had that hammer right now, I'd be hitting something, too."

He grabbed both her shoulders. "It's Marny who is in the wrong here, Ellie, not you. Mick and Marny have betrayed both our trusts."

Understanding filled her eyes. "It's LA all over again for you, isn't it? No wonder you were beating at that piece of metal as hard as you were."

"Maybe." In many ways it was, but there was another layer to this he hadn't had in LA. The pain of betrayal cut just as sharp, but now there was Ellie. Ellie understood how deep his hurt had cut, and could see things about him he'd lost the ability to view. She saw his gift as indestructible and invaluable when he'd thought it smashed beyond use. Against his will, and perhaps even without him realizing it, Ellie made him want to put himself out there again because Ellie was worth the pain. And even though Mick and Marny's betrayal hurt, he couldn't say he truly regretted doing the program. Not when it had brought him closer to Ellie.

"Look." He held her gaze, feeling the protector in him rise above the wound Mick had inflicted. "I will not let them hurt you. You or your family or your animals. I mean it. You have my word, Ellie." He allowed himself the luxury of pulling her toward him. She resisted for a moment and then laid that reluctance down. When she gave in and leaned against his chest, he could not have pulled back for all the world.

Nash felt her give a little shudder and then a big deep breath, as if fighting back a bout of tears. "I'm glad you're here," she said into his chest. Even as he told himself not to, he slipped his arms around her. He'd give the world to hold her tight and to tell her he would make it all okay, but he had no idea what the next hours held. Nor could he trust himself with her in this embittered state. He settled for a soft "I'm glad I'm here, too." And he was.

For the first time since he'd set foot in Martins Gap, Nash felt as if maybe God had sent him here to help Ellie, rather than simply run here in flight from himself.

The next hours flew by in a blur of conversations with Gunner and Gran, updates on searches for Marny and her father, and the various procedural events as the case unfolded. Finally, just as evening fell, Don and Nash called Gunner to let them know they had found Marny and her father and were bringing them to the sheriff's office for questioning.

Ellie insisted on going with Gunner. He'd argued at first, but Ellie dug in her heels until Gunner relented.

Now she stood with her brother outside the Martins Gap sheriff's office, steeling herself to go inside.

Nash stopped her at the curb. "You don't need to be here, Ellie. Gunner and I can handle this."

"I know that, but I want to be here." She looked up at him, touched by his continual efforts to protect her. Derek hadn't even bothered to protect her from the cameras that were all over the restaurant the day she had discovered his cheating. Every day Ellie discovered new ways Derek's charm had blinded her to his many shortcomings. *Thank You, Lord. I'm grateful we broke it off. That's Your healing.* Nash felt like part of God's healing, too. Someone to keep her safe while she put her heart back together. Someone who might very well steal that heart once it healed—and may have stolen it already. *It'd be a mistake to trust that pull toward him now. Not yet.* She squared her shoulders. "Would you have let Don question Mick without you?"

"Not a chance."

"I need to see her eyes, hear her voice. I need to try to understand why she'd do this."

He gave her a cautionary stare. "You may not get the answers you want, Ellie. You may be hurt by what you hear."

"What's one more hurt? I've had a target on my back for weeks now. I'm starting to feel armor plated."

"Some thick skins aren't worth having. Like I said, Don, Gunner and I can handle this. I doubt Jerry Fuller's going to be anything even close to kind in there."

"And like I said, I need to be here, even if it hurts."

She allowed herself a crack in the armor plating by adding, "But I wouldn't mind it if you stay close."

The request brought warmth to his eyes. "I'll do what I can, but I am on duty here. Just promise me if things get nasty you'll step outside and let us handle it."

"I've seen some impressive chef temper tantrums. I've learned when to duck." The small joke bolstered her confidence a bit. "No one in here has big knives and heavy pots, so I think I'll be okay."

The three of them walked into the sheriff's office, where Don already had set up chairs around a folding table. The tough edge Marny usually displayed seemed on its last legs, giving her face a twisted, tired appearance. Dark circles lurked under her eyes. She sat back in her chair, a forced posture of false calm as she thrust her long legs out in front of her, one ankle rocking back and forth. The ankle stilled when Marny caught sight of Ellie behind Gunner. Jerry Fuller, a thin man who shared Marny's sharp features on a hard-lined face, sat next to his daughter, his arms crossed over his chest in a defiance that visibly doubled when Gunner sat down. He looked as if he'd scoured the house for his last clean shirt.

Ellie stood behind Gunner and tried to catch Marny's eyes. The girl looked everywhere but in her direction.

Don folded his hands and cleared his throat in an official manner. "Jerry, do you give your consent for Marny here to be questioned about the events taking place on the Blue Thorn Ranch?"

"I do not."

Gunner gave a small growl while Don sighed and Nash leaned in.

"Now, Jerry, let's not make this harder than it has to be. Marny's young, and we all want to let cooler heads prevail, don't we?"

Based on the level of tension in the room, Ellie wondered if cool heads were even possible.

"I'll ask you again. Do you give your consent for us to question your daughter?"

"Dad." Marny spoke up, looking as if she was finally grasping the extent of her troubles.

"Fine," Jerry grumbled. "I consent. But if I hear anything I don't like—"

"You are welcome to call the questioning to a halt at any time," Don replied. "That's your right. But I'll repeat what I said when I called you in—information voluntarily given is in everyone's best interest here. Y'all stay calm and cooperate, and all this goes much easier."

They went on through an hour of facts, times and locations. Nash was right, learning the logistics of what had happened gave Ellie no satisfaction. The details told her all of the hows, but none of the whys. Every probe about Marny's motivation was met with a teenage shrug and an evasive "I dunno."

Yes, Marny and Mick had brought the rifle with them; no, they hadn't planned to kill an animal. Mr. Fuller hadn't put them up to it other than through endless rants—which he started on again until Don hushed him—that the Bucktons had ruined everyone's job prospects by exposing DelTex's crimes and thwarting the Ramble Acres development.

"Marny, can you explain exactly how you ended up

firing lethal shots into that bison?" Don asked, his pen poised over a notepad already filled with notations.

"You don't have to answer that, darlin'," Jerry said. "You don't have to answer nothin'."

It was then that Ellie finally succeeded in catching Marny's gaze. Ellie's own response to the suffocating indifference in the girl's eyes surprised her. *Help yourself*, Ellie found her heart calling to the young woman. *Push off this ugly bottom and start your climb up right now.*

"It was all so unfair, you know? Why do they get to be all righteous while the rest of us have to pay for it? Fancy yarn and picnics and all that baloney. You know what I got? I got no money, I can barely put gas in my car, and I got no time for stupid things like arts and crafts. All I got is Mick, and I won't have even him if I have to go to Waco and live with Mom. Only there's no money to keep me here, so I got no choice."

Ellie wondered if there would be sufficient funds if most of the Fullers' money didn't end up funding a bar tab at Lonesome's, but she kept that to herself. Nash's shoulders stiffened, and she knew he was harboring the same thought.

"If you think…" Gunner started, his own temper near boiling.

"Now, now," Don cautioned Gunner. "Let's let Marny tell us what she has to say. You'll get your say, I promise you that, but it ain't gonna be now."

"Go on, Marny," Nash said in a low voice.

"I wasn't shooting at anything at first. I just wanted

to make them run. The buffalo. Scare 'em like we did before. So at first I shot into the air over 'em."

"Where a bullet could come down anywhere in the herd?" Gunner interjected, planting his hands on the table.

"Don't you go—" Jerry started, rising in his chair.

"Gunner!" Don cut in sharply. "I will only allow you to stay as long as you can keep your temper. Is that clear?"

Ellie put a steadying hand on Gunner's shoulder. It was a good thing she was here, hard as it was.

"Then that one wandered right into my sights. An easy shot, right there. And I thought of everything that had happened and I thought, it'd feel good. I'd get to fight back just this one time. It all came boiling right up and into my trigger finger, and when he turned and gave me a clear shot right into his shoulder. After that shot he turned right at me, like he wasn't really that hurt and was daring me to stand my ground. Like he was saying 'Is that all you're gonna do?' or something. So I shot again into his chest. And when he went down, I didn't feel sad or nothing. There's almost a hundred of 'em anyways and only one of me. Felt like evening the score, I suppose."

Ellie couldn't decide if the lifeless tone of Marny's voice made it better or worse. Marny clearly realized the futility of what she'd done to make her life better—she was smart enough to see that it had, in fact, made her life worse. But it was as if all the time and attention and experiences Ellie had poured into Marny's life hadn't made the slightest bit of difference. Knitting? What had she been thinking? How could she be foolish enough to believe that yarn and needles could make any impact on these girls? Six weeks of pretty hobbies and nice snacks offered no real solutions to a father who couldn't put down the bottle long enough to hold a job. The whole enterprise seemed unrealistic and pointless. Nash was right: today wasn't going to provide any answers, only more doubts and questions.

When they charged Marny Fuller with criminal mischief and set her court date, Ellie waited for a sense of justice to settle her spirit.

It never came.

Chapter Seventeen

Ellie sat on the fallen tree trunk overlooking the little creek that ran through the back of Blue Thorn land. She'd adopted Gunner's favorite thinking spot since her return to the ranch, and when Nash had kept his promise to stop by after the day's formal proceedings with Marny, she'd taken him out here in hopes the peace of the surroundings would shake off the frustrations of the day for both of them.

From here she could see the herd as it stood peacefully in the next pasture, oblivious to the battle that had been waged over them and through them. Ellie realized how much she loved this place as the pain of Marny's misguided attack sank a little deeper. "She's just a confused kid making a poor choice, but it gets to me so."

Nash sat down beside her, his crisp uniform now replaced by a pair of worn jeans and mint-green shirt that made his striking hair stand out even more so. "It's tough to swallow someone setting out to hurt you. It sticks in your gut in the worst kind of way. Makes you second-guess everything."

He understood. Nash understood about the wound Derek had left in a way few other people had. She'd felt discarded by Derek, and that rejection had pulled the rug out from under the confidence she had always relied upon so deeply.

Gunner understood the pain of rejection and the betrayal that came from being cheated on—after all, he'd been in the same boat years back. But his sympathy was undermined by his only barely hidden opinion that the bison yarn enterprise was just a coping mechanism. Belittling her dream had been another blow to her self-esteem. Making yarn wasn't just a distraction; it was the implementation of an idea she'd harbored for two years. It was her unique way to contribute to the success of the Blue Thorn, and Gunner's dismissal of that stung hard on her raw spirit. Did anyone really believe in her anymore?

Ellie felt the tears she'd been holding back all day get the best of her. "I thought Marny and I were finally connecting. I know she was prickly and resistant, but I could see that was just an act. Marny was really taking to the knitting, and I liked that." After a pause and a wipe of her eyes, she added, "But I hadn't realized how much I liked that she was taking to me. Or at least, I thought she was."

Nash sighed. "She *was* taking to you. I think you're the first woman to pay any real attention to her in a long time. You showed her a Blue Thorn that wasn't the big, bad enemy. You nurtured a talent, a piece of herself that wasn't about merely surviving. When that wouldn't hold up against what she'd been hearing from her dad, I think the confusion took over her good sense."

It was funny, but Ellie's awareness snagged on Nash's use of the word *woman*. In countless small and unintentional ways, Ellie felt as though people still considered her a girl. Adele Buckton's granddaughter, Gunner and Luke's flighty sister, that nice girl from Texas at GoodEats. Being Derek Harding's fiancée had made her feel like a sophisticated city woman, the surprise contender able to settle down the bad-boy chef. And look how that had turned out. She wiped another streak of tears off one cheek with her shirtsleeve—an entirely too girl-like gesture, but she was fresh out of composure at the moment. Too tired of everything to be careful, she let her head fall on to Nash's shoulder.

He went perfectly still for a moment, and Ellie wondered if the gesture made him uncomfortable. After a moment, though, his hand came up to rest on her far shoulder, a careful hug of sorts. "I don't think she meant to hurt you or even your family. She meant to hurt the unfair world."

"The unfair world," Ellie echoed and sighed. "I can relate to that, I suppose."

"I'm sorry you got hurt," Nash said, his voice quiet but surprisingly strong. "I'm sorry for all of it. You're too fine a woman to be knocked down like this. It really is unfair."

She angled her head to look up at him, and something warm and trustworthy hummed between them. *You would not hurt me*, she thought, although she had nowhere near enough history or perspective to say that for a fact. It was a feeling, a heart-deep recognition. Being with Derek always had her buzzing with excitement, but this was something truer, more solid. She felt something for this man. Was it just her grasping at the first solid thing in a flood of rejection? Could she tell true feelings anymore?

She straightened up to look right at him, hoping to find a clue in his gaze. He was staring at her, and she could see it: the warmth and caution warring in his eyes. So he did feel it, just as she did. And he was as frightened of it as she was. "Nash," she said softly. "If you had met me in the middle of Los Angeles, would you have even noticed someone like me?"

She liked that he didn't just blurt out "Of course." He gave his answer thought, understood it for the request it was. "I'd have noticed you anywhere." There was a wonder in his voice that reached right down into the most broken corner of her heart. "I did notice," he continued. "On that very first night."

She felt her mouth curl up into a playful grin. "You noticed I was going eighty in a sixty-five zone."

"No," he said very softly, the single syllable saying a thousand things beyond the careful line they'd drawn between them. "That was just a fact. Numbers on a page. You, I noticed. Your eyes. The way you clung to the steering wheel, the way your hair was slipping out of the tangle you'd piled on top of your head."

She'd looked a mess that night, and she knew it. "And maybe the pile of Kleenex and biscotti next to me?"

He laughed, but it was a warm, low sound she could

feel in her chest. "Okay, that, too," he said, eyes bright despite the growing darkness around them. "But they only added to the charm."

They were too close, but she did not want to back away from him. "I'm a mess," she nearly whispered, a last attempt to discount the pull she felt toward this man and how probably neither of them should trust it.

Nash brought one finger up to run along a stray strand of her hair. "Maybe we're all messes. You, me, Marny, Mick—all of us."

Ellie let herself feel what his eyes did to her. The way he would not let more than one finger touch her hair. The way his other hand stayed so cautiously light on her shoulder. Ellie's heart warmed even more at the respect and honor his attitude conveyed. Derek had swung from wild infatuation to almost taking her for granted, and she'd convinced herself the wild ride was exciting. The truth was the wild ride had been exhausting. What she felt for this man was a deeper, steadier kind of care. She leaned in and heard his breath hitch as he put his hand out to stop her. She placed her hand over his and gently, cautiously kissed his cheek.

His whole body seemed to react. Something electric that blended among bliss and shock and release. Nash shifted and let his lips meet hers with an exquisite carefulness that made her feel anything but discarded. There were a million words to describe what that kiss felt like, but the one that struck her most deeply was *true*. Truth. She could still recognize it, still be touched by it.

He pulled back and looked at her with searching eyes, giving her every chance to stop what was happening between them. "I don't know how to be sure… It's all… I'm afraid I'll only hurt you," he confessed.

"Funny, I was just thinking the same thing," she replied as his thumb wiped a tear from her cheek. The gesture struck her with such reverence and tenderness that she kissed him. Deeply. Really, truly, deeply in a way that both healed her and terrified her at the same time. Everything was so fragile in the world, in danger of breaking apart at the slightest misstep.

He ended the kiss first, pulling just the smallest amount away, his eyes still closed as if he was dizzy from the contact. The smile that began in one corner of his mouth kindled in his eyes when he opened them. "Mayday," he groaned softly, making a pun on the day's date. "Officer down. That is exactly why I ought not to kiss you," he said in a husky voice. His hand returned to her cheek, his full hand now and not just one careful finger. "I don't know if I'm ready for that kind of wow."

Ellie found his frayed composure an honest, endearing compliment. "So what do we do now?"

"We go slow. We let things sort out. We hang on to what we know and find out what else we need to know." His fingers traced her chin and gently tipped it up toward him. "And one thing you need to know is that I will never hurt you. I will keep you safe, even from me." He turned her shoulders so that she leaned against him and together they stared out at the pastures rather than at each other. *Only this far for now*, his gesture said, and as Ellie leaned back against this solid, steady man, she found his gesture even more romantic than the kiss.

Can I trust what I'm feeling? Is my heart strong

enough yet to be safe? Yet when she was with Nash, safe was exactly how she felt.

"I thought I ran here for no particular reason," she offered. "I don't think I let myself realize how much I'd wanted to come back."

"Didn't you want to come back before?"

"I think I felt like I couldn't be the person I'd become if I came back here. I'd just be young, silly Elllie with the pie-in-the-sky dreams. I think to Gunner—and maybe even to Gran—I still am that girl."

"You're not a girl," Nash said quietly. She could feel his breath catch behind her, and she gave quiet thanks that she could not be caught up in whatever she knew she would see in his eyes. "You are a beautiful, amazing woman."

"I'm not so sure Gunner sees it that way."

"Gunner thinks you don't see things through. He's afraid you'll launch this yarn thing and then leave him with the pieces." Nash straightened, then turned her to face him again. "Is he right?"

"No." Ellie took Nash's hands. "Well, if this were the old me—the me who left for Atlanta—then I suppose I'd have to say I don't know. But I'm different now. I stick with things now. Which is what makes it so hard. I want to stick with GoodEats and follow through on my commitments there, but I don't know if anyone will ever take me seriously after everything that's happened. And I want to stick with the Blue Thorn—" she raised one hand to touch his face "—and other things that are here. Only I'm not sure I can."

Nash paused for a long moment. "You'll have to choose eventually."

"I know."

He clasped her hand and squeezed it tightly. "It doesn't have to be now. Maybe it shouldn't be now. Maybe when we're less of a mess, we'll know what to do."

"About this?"

"About everything."

Chapter Eighteen

Ellie pushed the enter button on her laptop with a flourish. "There," she pronounced to the room. "The Blue Thorn Fibers online store is officially up and running. Phase one is complete. And three days before my September first deadline—I'm ahead of schedule."

"Oh, we've got phases and schedules now, do we?" Gunner commented from his seat on the couch.

She turned around in the office chair to face the room. Gunner, a due-any-day-now Brooke and Audie filled the couch, while Gran applauded from a side chair. Nash, too fidgety to sit down, had alternated between pacing near the wall by the windows and leaning against the bookshelves.

"Well, I've still got to pay the bills working at the Austin Restaurateurs Association until the actual shop is up and running," she answered her brother. "You've never had a retail arm of Blue Thorn. You have no idea how much work running a place like that can be. We definitely need to ramp things up slowly."

"Bison meat, bison leather goods and bison yarn all in one shop?" Gunner raised an eyebrow. "You're sure this is going to work?"

She'd explained the business plan to Gunner a dozen times now and had begun conversations with their cousin Witt to come on board to run the retail meat business. "Yes, Gunner, it will," she declared, determined to keep the frustration from her voice. It had taken her all summer to figure out what was next in her life, but now she was jumping into it with both feet— and a smart plan. She refused to be stymied by Gunner's nagging doubts. "The ranch is doing well, but it could still do better. This gives us two additional income streams *and* increased visibility."

Gran gave Gunner a look. "How many times are you going to make her convince you? We all voted yes. Now let the girl get on with things."

Ellie looked over to Nash for a show of support, but he seemed to be preoccupied with his smartphone.

Brooke peered at the computer screen. "The website sure is nice looking. I had no idea Robby was so talented."

Ellie waited for Nash to reply to that, but the man's head was still bent over his phone. She tamped down her annoyance and spoke up herself. "Well, he wasn't that great as a car guy, but once Nash got him on the computer we found out where his real skills lie. He took to website design like a fish to water, didn't he, Nash?"

Nash grunted and nodded, but didn't look up. Something must have been wrong—he'd been so loving and attentive since she'd moved to an apartment halfway between Martins Gap and Austin, spending all his free time on the weekends with her either there or here on the ranch. In the past six months her entire life had righted itself into a splendid new future. *I thought I knew love with Derek, but You've given me a man who shows me what true love is. Thank You, Lord.*

"Are you serious about hiring Marny once the store is open?" Gran asked. "I know you've patched things up between you, but are you sure?"

"We'll need some help, and I want her to have a future here in Martins Gap. Besides, she's one talented knitter—and so fast. I told her she could sell hand-knitted bison socks on commission and you should have seen how her eyes lit up." It had taken a lot of prayer and communication to get to the heart of Marny's anger and helplessness. Ellie considered her repaired relationship with the girl to be one of the greatest achievements of her reshaped new life. Yes, Marny had hurt her, but they'd moved past it, and now Ellie truly wanted her to succeed. If working in the Blue Thorn Shop once it opened helped that to happen, then Ellie was all for it. "I only wish Mick would come back." With only a misdemeanor criminal mischief on his record, Mick had enlisted in the military shortly after graduation. "I hope he gets himself straightened out."

"If he can't do it on his own, the army will likely do it for him," Gunner remarked. "I think it may have been the best thing for the guy. He may sorely miss his father's inattention by the end of boot camp, but all that supervision should do him a world of good."

"We'll see." Ellie stared hard at Nash, his inattention

getting under her skin. Launching the online store for Blue Thorn Fibers was a big deal for her—why was he tapping away on his phone?

Her irritation was cut short by a *ding* from the computer. "Look at that! Only up and running for fifteen minutes and already we have our first sale!"

"Hooray for Aunt Ellie!" Audie cheered, running up to throw her arms around Ellie and plant a big sloppy kiss on her aunt's cheek. "What'd they buy? What'd they buy?"

Ellie opened the transaction section of her website software to bring up the order. "Eight skeins of Blue Thorn wool and bison blend. And guess what color, Audie?"

"Russet!" Audie pointed to the screen that showed the small selection of available colors. No one ever doubted the natural color of the bison yarn would get any other name than Russet. The burly calf Audie had named—now a full-grown adult—had become as much a Blue Thorn fixture as his mother, Daisy.

"Oh, look," Ellie said, scrolling through the rest of the order. "They ordered the men's sweater pattern, too."

"Where are they from?" Audie asked. "Can you tell?"

Ellie punched the few keys that brought up the customer information, then froze. She spun in the chair, only to find herself staring into the face of her first customer. "You?"

"Why not?" said Nash, who now stood right next to her. "You've never made me anything before."

Ellie felt her cheeks flush. "You know why."

Nash got the oddest look on his face as he pulled her up out of the chair. "Well, now you can just make it after."

"After what?"

"After we get married." He fished into his pocket and got down on one knee. Ellie felt the room spin, barely hearing Audie's delighted whoops and cheers. "You said it's okay after. I just think of it as a down payment. Well, that, and this." He produced the most exquisite ring: a round white diamond hugged on either side by swirls of tiny blue sapphires—similar to, but wonderfully different from the family heirloom Brooke wore on her finger. Ellie's heart burst in a million directions as she watched Nash slip the ring on her finger. It was perfect. She loved it. She loved him. She stared at it, then at him, her heart so filled with joy it felt as if she couldn't hope to produce breath or words.

She felt something bump up against her hips. "Aunt Ellie," Audie whispered loudly. "You're supposed to say yes."

Nash's hand came up to touch her cheek in the way that always made her knees buckle. "That is sort of what I am hoping for."

It was as if all the *yeses* in the world fought to get there first—speech felt entirely beyond possible. Instead, she began to laugh and cry and nod furiously all at the same time as she threw her arms around Nash's neck, holding him like the lifeline he'd become.

"Looks like yes to me." Gran laughed.

Nash kissed her, then said "I love you" softly into her

ear, sending tingles zipping out through her fingertips. He kissed her again. "You saved me."

It was what they had come to say to each other over the summer—a promise, a ritual between them. "You saved me," she said, marveling at the ring on her finger and the purely perfect state of the world. "My hero."

"Grow old with me right here in Martins Gap." His arms slipped around her waist and she forgot anyone else was even in the room. "You can knit me a sweater and bake me biscotti every year until I'm eighty."

"Every year until you're ninety, Natsuhito," she corrected. "And maybe a few more years after that."

"Not-so *what*-o?" Audie balked.

Ellie would have explained, but she was too busy— her future husband was giving her the world's most perfect kiss.

* * * * *

Dear Reader,

Life loves to throw us a curve, doesn't it? The event we are sure spells disaster can often be the door to something so much better. We may plan one move, only to discover God has something altogether different in mind. The life of faith isn't always a "fun" adventure, but it is always for our good—even when we can't see it.

If this is your first visit to the Blue Thorn Ranch, I invite you to go back and meet Gunner Jr. in the series' previous book, *The Texas Rancher's Return*. You'll also be delighted to know Gunner and Ellie's cousin Witt gets his story next, with the Buckton younger twin siblings, Luke and Tess, to follow after.

As always, I love to hear from you. Email me at allie@alliepleiter.com, visit my website at www.alliepleiter.com or find me on Facebook and Twitter.

Blessings,

REQUEST YOUR FREE BOOKS!

2 FREE INSPIRATIONAL NOVELS
PLUS 2
FREE
MYSTERY GIFTS